01/2019

BOWEN ISLAND LIBRARY
3 0947 0005 4843 4

DISCARDED

D0041911

Bowen Island Public Library

WHAT BLOWS UP

Ted Staunton

Illustrations by Britt Wilson

Scholastic Canada Ltd.
Toronto New York London Auckland Sydney
Mexico City New Delhi Hong Kong Buenos Aires

To an awesome Epic Squad:
Richard, Lesley, Kevin, Britt, Anne and Erin
— T.S.

Scholastic Canada Ltd.
604 King Street West, Toronto, Ontario M5V 1E1, Canada

Scholastic Inc.
557 Broadway, New York, NY 10012, USA

Scholastic Australia Pty Limited
PO Box 579, Gosford, NSW 2250, Australia

Scholastic New Zealand Limited
Private Bag 94407, Botany, Manukau 2163, New Zealand

Scholastic Children's Books
Euston House, 24 Eversholt Street, London NW1 1DB, UK

www.scholastic.ca

Library and Archives Canada Cataloguing in Publication
Staunton, Ted, 1956-, author
    What blows up / Ted Staunton ; illustrated by Britt Wilson.

(The almost epic squad)
Issued in print and electronic formats.
ISBN 978-1-4431-5782-7 (hardcover).--ISBN 978-1-4431-5783-4 (ebook)

    I. Wilson, Britt, 1986-, illustrator II. Title.

PS8587.T334W43 2019   jC813'.54   C2018-904825-5
                                                C2018-904826-3

Illustrations and hand lettering by Britt Wilson.
Cover background image copyright © Piotrurakau/Getty Images.

Text copyright © 2019 by Ted Staunton.
Illustrations copyright © 2019 by Scholastic Canada Ltd.
All rights reserved.
No part of this publication may be reproduced or stored in a retrieval system, or transmitted in any form or by any means, electronic, mechanical, recording, or otherwise, without written permission of the publisher, Scholastic Canada Ltd., 604 King Street West, Toronto, Ontario M5V 1E1, Canada. In the case of photocopying or other reprographic copying, a licence must be obtained from Access Copyright (Canadian Copyright Licensing Agency), 56 Wellesley Street West, Suite 320, Toronto, Ontario M5S 2S3 (1-800-893-5777).

6 5 4 3 2 1   Printed in Canada 114   19 20 21 22 23

4

5

NOTHING REMAINS BUT THE STENCH OF SCORCHED RUBBER-SOLED NURSING SHOES.

...OR SO IT SEEMS...

DR. FASSBINDER AND HIS ASSISTANTS CONTINUE THEIR EXPERIMENTS IN A TOP-SECRET LAB IN MONTREAL, TESTING THE CHILDREN FOR "GIFTED" EVERY YEAR...

MEANWHILE, SOMEONE KNOWN ONLY AS "THE BOSS" QUIETLY RECRUITS A TEAM OF NEFARIOUS MINIONS TO SHADOW THE ALMOST EPIC KIDS...

...AND TAKES TO THE SKIES IN A TATTERED BLIMP. EVER ANGRY, EVER EVIL, EVER SMELLING OF BURNT RUBBER, AND IMPATIENTLY AWAITING THE CHILDREN AND THEIR POWERS.

BUT WHAT OF THE CHILDREN TODAY?

8

CHAPTER 1

CLOWN AROUND

"I think we're being followed," Kirsten Lundborg said as the Métro doors closed. The train started moving.

"Huh?" said her brother, Gary. Gary said that a lot. He'd been distracted by a blurry poster about basketball. It reminded him of his one basket of the school season.

"Remember that creepy clown giving away fries coupons outside the hotel?"

"Sure, I've got them right here," said their mom.

"Um . . ." Gary said. No, he didn't remember. He'd been too busy wishing that his pants were longer. He looked at his sister. Kirsten was blurry too. Or was it his glasses? Gary polished them on his jersey.

Kirsten went on, "Well, the same clown was outside the subway. And now he's on the train. Don't look!"

Gary couldn't. Without glasses everything was even blurrier. He put them back on. Everything was still blurry. *What the . . . ?* He remembered the mayonnaise incident at lunch. *Ohhhh, yeah.* He took off his glasses and polished again.

"Hon," Mrs. Lundborg said, "I'm sure Nemesis Burgers has more than one clown. It's a promotional thing."

"Mom, the guy is *panting.* He raced after us, I know it."

Their mom laughed. "You're reading too many mysteries."

Gary put his glasses on and saw that beside him a man in a business suit was playing a game on his phone, his thumbs dancing across the screen. Two dragons were about to incinerate a warrior swinging a sword.

"Chop the third spike on their tails," Gary blurted. *Click, click*; thumbs flew. The dragons disintegrated. "I bet there's extra Health in that tree," Gary said. *Click, click, click.* There was.

The man looked up. "Awesome, dude. Thanks! You've played this one?"

Gary beamed. AwesomeDude27 was what he'd picked for his gamer name.

"Nah," he said, "but one kind of like it. I just get a . . . feeling." Things like this had happened all his life, especially lately. He just wished he could use it more himself. Since his latest growth spurt had begun, Gary's own thumbs had been as nimble as two logs in a mud pit, which was why his gamer name had actually come out as AsseomeDud27.

"Gary," Kirsten nudged him, "our stop."

From the subway, they walked to a big hospital

Gary never remembered the name of. A clown with a purple hat and green hair hurried up to the corner.

"See?" Kirsten insisted.

"Huh?"

The Lundborgs rode an elevator to a dingy corridor in the hospital's sub-basement. At the end was a door with something like a miniature cat flap at the bottom and a sign reading *Institut de l'ennui / Boredom Institute* near the top. Above it, a light flickered ominously.

"Looks like a job for Dimly Bulb," Mrs. Lundborg cracked. She made the same joke every visit.

Inside, the Boredom Institute matched its name, with a dusty waiting room and a hallway leading to more doors with little flaps. As usual, it smelled of cheese. Gary signed in. Like yesterday, there was one other name on the sheet: *A. O'Kaye.*

"Okay, bud," said Mrs. Lundborg. "We'll be back at four to see Doctor F. Text if you'll be longer." She and Kirsten were on their annual shopping trip. Montreal had more to offer than Dimly, Manitoba.

"You watch. That clown will still be there," Kirsten said.

"Good," said Mrs. Lundborg. "We'll get more coupons."

They left. Gary turned and bumped a chair, which

knocked a table. A pile of magazines slid to the floor. He bent to pick them up and hit his head on the chair. Gary sat down, rubbed the sore spot, and sighed.

Until now, he'd had one of his feelings this might be his year for gifts. In the past it hadn't bothered him that Dr. Fassbinder's testing never found anything; the Lundborgs still got a free trip to Montreal. Gary and his dad had even seen a Canadiens playoff game. A couple of other kids from Dimly, Jess Flem and her friend, *ummmmm* — Gary hunted for her name — *Daisy*, the hippie-dippy one who'd moved away a while back, did the tests too, and he didn't think they'd changed either. Now Gary wanted gifts. Big time. His growth spurt had earned him a new nickname: Clumsborg. This was not as cool as Awesome Dude, to say the least.

Gary suspected he wouldn't be so klutzy if he concentrated more, but it was hard to remember to concentrate. It wasn't that he didn't think, it was just that he was usually thinking about the wrong things. And when his thinking did click, or he got that feeling like today on the subway, he was too clumsy to do anything about it.

Go, gifts! Gary thought, looking at the mayo stains on his shirt. He wasn't asking for superpowers here, just to, say, pass math and outshoot Kirsten at twenty-one. Which reminded Gary of his one-basket season again.

All year, he'd thought *Score, Score, Score* and fumbled every chance. Then, in the final game, the Dimly Bulbs vs. the Polonia Panthers, the Polonians had been chanting "Prowl, Panthers!" *Prowl*, Gary thought as he waved his hands on defence, and he got one of his feelings.

He'd spun straight into a Panther pass that bounced off his chest and downcourt. The other players were so surprised that they'd simply watched as Gary chased it down and launched a desperation buzzer-beater as he tripped over his own feet. The ball had rattled around the rim before finally, reluctantly, dropping. Gary had sailed on into his principal, who was wearing the school's light bulb mascot costume. They'd both broken their glasses.

Not only had he won the game, but he'd gotten new and cooler glasses out of it. Gary pushed them up his nose. He yanked tissues from a box on the table, scrunched them, and stood to fire a jumper at the wastebasket. His shot missed. He took more tissues and kept on missing.

From somewhere, a voice crooned, "Lookin' smoooooth there. That juke to the right? *Sweet.*"

"Huh?" Gary stumbled. An eerily tidy boy about his own age stood in the hall. Something in the kid's voice made Gary believe him instantly, despite the tissue snowdrift on the floor. "Gee, thanks."

The boy hopped nimbly over the magazines Gary hadn't picked up. "You," the buttery tones wafted, "could be a three-point king." Then, before Gary's eyes, his hair frazzled, his shirttail popped out, and he snapped, "If you had any talent. Call that a shot? I've seen better at the flu clinic." He left, slamming the door.

Behind Gary, another voice drawled, "Pitter patter, let's get at 'er." It was Dr. Fassbinder.

CHAPTER 2

CRUMB OF HOPE

Dr. Fassbinder was a plump man in orange sneakers. Today, as always, he sported a ponytail, a big upswept moustache and one of his many Grateful Dead T-shirts under his lab coat. He too smelled of cheese.

"C'mawn in, Gary." His accent stretched *"Ga-aa-ry"* into three syllables. "Yesterday's test results were normal, kiddo. Let's see what today brings."

First came a memory test Gary didn't remember. Then he had to build something out of toothpicks and foam cups. It collapsed. What had he been thinking about? Oh, yeah: *Clumsborg.*

They took a break. Up in the cafeteria, Gary, who was perpetually hungry these days, had chocolate milk, a tuna sandwich and a doughnut. Dr. F. nibbled a cheddar croissant. Cheese crumbs clung to his abundant moustache.

Gary said, "If you ate that with the cheese side down, you wouldn't get bits in your moustache."

"Wha—? You know, Gary, that's a good idea." Dr. F. brushed at his face. "I should have thought of that myself. Did you work that out or—"

"I just got this feeling I get sometimes."

"That's called intuition: understanding something without thinking it through, just 'getting' it. You've always tested as very intuitive. It's a good thing to have." Dr. F. nibbled more croissant, cheese side down this time. "So, Gare, speaking of 'feeling things,' have you ever, uhhhh, had the feeling you were being followed?"

"Huh?" Gary swallowed. "My sister did, but she doesn't like clowns."

Dr. F. raised an eyebrow. "Let me put it another way: Have you ever noticed anyone watching you?"

"Oh. Yeah." Gary sighed. "All the time."

Dr. F. leaned in. "Who?"

Gary felt his face redden. "Everybody at school. They want to see how I'm going to klutz-out next."

"Riiiight. Okay, how about blimps? Ever seen one around Dimly?"

"We call our science teacher Mr. Blimp because he's—"

"What say we get back to work?" Dr. F. stood up. Crumbs spilled from his lap.

In the sub-basement, they passed a laundry cart. A purple hat lay in one corner. Where had Gary seen that before? Ahead, someone in coveralls stood on a ladder, tinkering with the flickering light. It looked to be a teenage girl wearing a men's wig and a fake moustache.

"Maintenance. Won't be long," she muttered. Dr. F. nodded without looking up from his phone.

A heat shield had been set up in the testing room. This was something new. Dr. F. held a piece of paper in front of it with fireplace tongs. "See if you can burn a hole in this with laser vision."

"Huh?"

By the time Kirsten and Mrs. Lundborg returned, Gary had failed tests for every superpower ever found in comics or movies. This had to be his last visit, he thought. For once, his — what had Dr. Fassbinder called it? Oh yeah, intuition — for once, his intuition had failed. He was going to be Clumsborg forever.

"No clowns," Kirsten reported.

"Glad they've finally fixed your light," said Mrs. Lundborg. "So, how did it go?"

They all sat in Dr. F.'s office. He shrugged. "Upside: Gary is a healthy, normal kid. Growing like a weed, which is affecting his coordination just now. And very intuitive. We've always known he thinks in interesting ways. Downside: His gifts are still . . . unclear. We've been testing in the afternoons because I hoped the time of his birth, 1:47 p.m., might be important, especially this year, now he's hitting puberty. It doesn't seem to be the case."

"Gary wasn't born at 1:47 p.m.," Mrs. Lundborg said. "It was 1:47 *a.m.*"

Dr. Fassbinder shot up from his chair. Being short, it was not that far. "Are you sure?"

"Trust me, I was there. All fourteen hours. Must be a typo on the file."

"Of course. Sorry. But this changes everything. Gary has to come back tonight."

"We're going to the movies," Gary said, even though he felt a spark of hope.

"After, then. Even better. We'll extend your stay. There's room in the budget."

"Cool," said Kirsten.

Mrs. Lundborg pursed her lips. "Well," she said, "school *is* almost over." She looked at Gary. He nodded. "Fine," she said. "We'll drop him off after the movie, but he has to do his math homework first."

CHAPTER 3

LABBERGASTED

It was past 2:00 a.m. when Gary nodded off in the testing room. The movie he'd seen earlier had featured a lot of swooping starfighter craft. Maybe that was why he dreamed the fireplace tongs from the afternoon's testing were sailing around the light fixtures, battling flying tissue boxes.

Noises jerked him awake: shouting, crashes, a thud, then a cascade of something falling around him. Gary blinked. Bits of plaster and pebbled plastic were scattered at his feet. Water pattered on his head. Gary looked up. One of the light fixtures dangled in front of him, swaying by a wire. The tongs were rammed into the ceiling, a tissue box impaled on each arm. Tissues wafted like spring snowflakes in Dimly.

The sprinkler system had kicked in as well. Amid it all, Dr. Fassbinder was shouting orders to mice in tiny lab coats.

Huh?

Dr. F. pushed past the light fixture and pumped Gary's hand. His moustache danced wildly. "You did it, Gary! Congratulations!" A tissue settled on the doctor's head. He didn't seem to notice.

"Huh?"

Behind Dr. F., mice were swivelling a video camera

recording the destruction. "*You* did *this*!" cried Dr. F.

"Geez, sorry. I don't—"

"No, it's wonderful! Gary, your powers have kicked in. You must have—" Dr. F. took a deep breath. "Gary, try this. See that chair? Move it." Gary rose. Dr. F. stopped him. "No, with your mind. *Will* it to move."

"You mean, like, um, tele-whatsit?"

"Telekinesis. Exactly. Imagine moving it."

Dr. F. didn't seem to be kidding. Gary eyed the chair. It looked heavy. He pushed up his glasses, sucked in a breath, and summoned a big mental push. *Now.* The chair rocketed across the room and bashed into the wall. Mice squeaked and leaped to safety, lab coats billowing like superhero capes.

Gary's mouth opened. At first nothing came out. "Wow," he finally breathed. "Sorry, I forgot the . . . roller thingies . . ."

"Never mind." Dr. F. reverently patted the dented wall. "My friends, success!"

The mice broke into applause. A tiny voice cried, "Bravo!" This was followed by an angry squeak. Dr. Fassbinder lifted his sneaker from a mouse tail.

"Sorry, Elaine. C'mon, everybody. To the lab."

The mice hustled through the door flap. Gary and Dr. Fassbinder followed in the regular way. Behind another door was a room Gary had never seen before: a laboratory, bustling with mice scampering on computer keyboards, lugging test tubes, and wiring connections.

"They're nocturnal," said the doctor, as if that was all that needed explaining.

Other than that, it wasn't much of a lab. The computers were old, the work tables cluttered. There was a microwave, refrigerators labelled *cheese* and *brain samples* and a lounge area with dollhouse furniture. There, two mice were putting marbles on a *mini* minigolf course, another stood over a sudoku chewing a pencil, and one bench-pressed a wrench. In a far corner sat cardboard boxes marked *DIMLY BULB: The Light of Your Life.*

"Do you know what reidium is, Gary?"

Gary thought. "Um, is it when you're bored with reading?"

Dr. F.'s eyebrows bunched and his moustache drooped. Gary imagined it sweeping up again. The hairs shot skyward.

"OW!"

"Sorry."

"Not to worry." The doctor paused for a moment, gingerly patting his moustache. "No, Gary, reidium is a rare element, a hyperconductor." He nodded at the boxes. "It was used in light filaments and systems made in your hometown, until it was declared too volatile. But it's special for another reason too. When my assistants here were babies, I exposed them to reidium. Look at them now. You were accidentally exposed to reidium, Gary, in the Dimly hospital just after you were born. And now you have special power too." He took something from his pocket. "Cheese?"

Gary blinked. *What was going on?* All he'd wanted was a little coordination, maybe some math smarts. "No, thank you. Could I have a glass of water?"

"Sure, there are beakers by the sink. Use your power . . . On second thought, let me get it."

The mice took a cheese break, then patched Gary with sensors. Machines beeped and hummed as he guided balloons (tricky), printed on a whiteboard (very tricky), and threw darts (don't ask) using mind power. Then came a couple of accidental don't-asks involving a tennis racquet and a Bunsen burner. Gary quickly thought the fire extinguisher into action. Unfortunately his glasses had come off. He aimed at the wrong place and destroyed some computers.

"Not to worry," said Dr. F. "They were old ones."

"Everything in this dump is old," squeaked a voice.

It was all so strange that it was hard to concentrate. After a while Gary's power began fading. By 6:00 a.m. it was gone. He slumped sootily in a tangle of wires. Thirteen years of waiting for three hours of mental

*Clumsborg*ing. It hardly seemed fair. At least his feeling had been right.

"Don't worry," said Dr. F., nibbling now-smoked cheese. "It's probably a cycle; your power should return. We'll test again tomorrow night. Now you need some rest. Tell no one. I'll talk to your mom."

"We'll get a budget increase!" cheered a mouse peeling off Gary's sensor stickers.

"Budget, schmudget," groused the voice Gary had heard complaining earlier. The mouse was coated in foam from the fire extinguisher. "We should be a reality series. That's where the money is. We'd be stars! Millionaires!"

"Claude, this is pure science! Research is its own reward," sighed Dr. Fassbinder.

The argument was raging when Gary left. In the cab he messaged Jess back in Dimly: "Weirdest visit with dr F evr! We should talkl." Then he fell asleep.

The second night Gary's power came and went again. There were more don't-asks, this time with barbells, a TV remote and the microwave.

"Your cycle is 3:00 a.m. to 6:00 a.m.," panted a mouse as it hopped on laptop keys, entering the data.

"And you have to clearly see what you are doing," chimed another, scrubbing red stains on a counter. There were a lot of red stains around the lab.

"And eating garlic boosts your power during the cycle," said a third, plugging in a vacuum cleaner.

Gary burped. There had been a lot of Caesar salad.

"And you could try *concentrating*," complained Claude, the mouse who wanted to be on reality TV. He was raking up broken glass with a fork.

Gary had peeled off his own sensors this time. "Sorry about the mess. Let me help." He switched on the vacuum. It sucked up two mice standing in front of the nozzle. Gary hit the *off* button and yanked out the bag. Dirt flew. The mice plopped out, coughing and spluttering. "SORRY!" Gary yelped.

Dr. F. flapped a hand, partly to avoid the dust cloud and partly to wave away Gary's garlic breath. "Forget it. You meant well. Marvin and Denise, you two okay? Just an accident." The mice coughed and waved.

"Yeah, but I mean about the other stuff, like the—"

"Gary, how would you know we had tomato sauce in the microwave?"

"I thought it was just garlic bread."

"You're a telekinetic wrecking crew." Claude waved his fork.

"Enough," said Dr. F. "Gary is trying."

"What happens now?" Gary asked, stepping over Claude and the glass.

"First you get some breath mints," said Dr. F. "Then you go back to Dimly. You are officially Top Secret, even from your parents. I'll explain to them. You'll get a call from Department C, a man named Cheeper. He'll use a password." The doctor leaned in and whispered, *"Tapioca."* He straightened. "Got that?" Gary nodded. "Excellent. You'll have training this summer. More garlic before you go? Cheese?"

"No thanks."

"Don't worry, Gary. This is new and strange, but your coordination will catch up to your growth and your power. In the meantime, practise, if you can stay awake. Eat lots of garlic. And try to concentrate, huh?"

They skirted the smoking ruin of a TV set. A barbell stuck out of the screen. At the door, Dr. F. shook Gary's hand. Gary felt a piece of paper being slipped to him.

Out in the hall he looked at it: *Watch for blimps* it read. Gary burped again. Overhead, the light began to flicker.

CHAPTER 4

GREY-GREEN AND CRUSTY

Two days later Gary rode his skateboard down Albert Street. It was his second trip home from school; the first trip home he'd forgotten to bring his backpack.

Dimly was flat and Albert was the only street with enough slope to ride, even slowly. Slow was fine if you were Clumsborging. It felt good to rest on the board in his new size twelve zebra-striped Con Airs. Gary was tired. Secretly practising your superpower at three in the morning really took it out of a guy, especially if you had to be up at seven for school.

Still, Gary was working on his concentration. He remembered to lean just so into a nifty turn onto Hoagland Avenue, then got one of his feelings.

Unfortunately, this was not a good one. An instant later — "Aaah!" — he was airborne. For a heartbeat, Gary thought he had a new superpower. Then he came down hard, on his butt. At first he thought he'd hit a patch of ice. Dimly in spring was mosquitoes one day and snow the next.

Shoving back his glasses, Gary saw he'd landed on a crusted pile of . . . gunk. His skateboard was jammed nose-first into the outer edge. Swarms of insects struggled fitfully on the waxy surface. Gary felt it giving way beneath him. He scrambled up as his Con Airs broke through and disappeared in a mass of slime. Gary flailed. The stuff clutched at him. Already it was crusting around his ankles, trapping him.

A Dimly Works Department tanker truck rolled down Hoagland and stopped in front of him. His dad, who ran the department, was driving. He and one of the crew climbed from the cab.

"Hang on, Gare," said Mr. Lundborg. "We'll have you out in a jiff." The men coupled a hose to the tanker and turned on the compressor. A second later a blast of water shot Gary free. Gobs of grey-green gunk splattered everywhere. Gary sloshed back to his skateboard.

"Thanks, Dad. What *is* that stuff?"

"Beats me." Mr. Lundborg tilted back his feed&seed cap. "We were helping get the SynthetICE down at Dimly Field when we got the call. It's the third one we've cleaned up this week. Anyway, it's not toxic; we tested. Really soak it down," he said to the other worker. "Otherwise it'll clog the storm drain. Get on home and grab a good hot shower, Gare. I'll see you at supper."

Kirsten was home from her Ultimate Frisbee game, eating a bowl of cereal, when Gary clumped into the kitchen after his shower. "What happened to you?" she asked. Gary's ruined tuque and Con Airs lay dripping on the back doormat.

"I flipped out into this pile of . . . stuff over on Hoagland."

"Stuff?"

"Yeah, all grey-green and crusty, with mosquitoes in it. Slime, kind of."

"Eeew," Kirsten said. "TMI. I'm eating here."

Gary was still thinking about the puddle. "Like snot."

"*GARE!* TMI. Geez. And not too close with the garlic breath, okay?"

"Huh? Oh, sorry. But it was like snot. Like Jess Flem exploded, or something." Jess was plagued with allergies. Mostly she hung out in her basement and played *Gang of Greats*, where she annihilated Gary — well, AsseomeDud27 — regularly.

Romeo, the family cat, padded past them. He paused, seeing the milk carton on the counter. "Forget it, Romeo," Kirsten said. Then to Gary, "I'm glad you didn't let him catch that mouse last night."

Romeo had been tormenting a mouse when they'd snuck downstairs the night before. Gary had levitated it from the cat's paws and scooted it outside when Kirsten opened the door. Saving the mouse was the only useful thing Gary had done with his superpower, besides making peanut-butter-and-garlic sandwiches. In Dimly there wasn't a lot to do at four in the morning, even with telekinesis, and especially if your parents didn't know you were up.

Kirsten was the only one who knew his secret. The family had been told Gary had made "*a promising neuro-psychokinetic adaptive transference breakthrough*," whatever that meant, and that he'd be invited to "gifted camp." Grandparents were excited. Kirsten, though, had caught him playing no-hands *Gang of Greats* one night.

Kirsten finding out had been a good thing. Her cool helped keep him focused, especially on tricky things, and Gary now felt ready to aim higher. The plan for tonight was to levitate their dad's Works Department key ring from the dresser, so they could sneak down and let themselves into the Dimly Community Centre. Then Gary could try shooting hoops with telekinesis.

"I still say that mouse swore as it went by me," Kirsten said. "This raspy little voice. He said—"

"No way," Gary interrupted.

"You told me the mice at the lab could talk."

"But they had reidium. They weren't just random mice in Dimly."

"So how did they get redium?"

"Dr. F. gave it to them."

Kirsten pressed, "But how?"

"Huh? I dunno. It doesn't matter."

"Maybe it does. You got yours sprinkled on your spine, right?"

"Yeah. When I was a baby. I told you. Dr. F. said that's how it got into my, uh, central nervous system."

"Well, that happened here. There's reidium in Dimly. It *could* happen, Gare." Kirsten turned away to rinse her empty bowl in the sink. "Like, what if some random person around here, say, had a broken blister and *stepped* in reidium?"

Gary shrugged. "When they were a baby? Babies can't walk."

"No, Gare. That's not—"

They were interrupted by two things at once. One was their mom, home from work with pizza (Tuesdays were pizza night for the Lundborgs; Gary had asked for extra garlic). The other was the phone. Gary answered.

A clipped voice said, "Gary Lundborg, please."

"Huh? Speaking."

"Bernard Cheeper here, Department C. Do you want some *tapioca*?"

"Huh? No thanks. I'm having dinner soon."

"Are you sure? *TAPIOCA?*"

"Ohhhhhhhh," Gary remembered. "Okay. But not much, we're having pizza."

"Pardon? Ah, I get your point; this may not be a secure line," said Cheeper, "and long-distance calls are expensive. Gary, things are moving faster than we thought. Big developments. Your country — in fact, the world — needs you now. Training camp starts tomorrow."

"But we have a field trip at school tomorrow. We're going to the . . . um . . . flood museum in Winnipeg."

"Maybe I should speak to your parents," said Cheeper.

Thirty minutes later Gary was chewing extra-garlic pizza and stuffing underwear in his backpack, along with his Dimly Bulb logo jerseys, bought cheap last month from the Precious Seconds consignment store in town. The jerseys were Gary's favourites because the graphic was the same as his school basketball team's.

Out the window he could see a dot on the horizon. Or was it on his glasses? He cleaned them. Nope. The dot was larger now: a fat cigar shape, trailing smoke. Hadn't he read something about blimps lately?

Gary shrugged. It didn't matter. He was off to training camp to learn to use his power. The world needed him, and even better, he was getting time off school. How cool was that? No more Clumsborging now.

His mom was climbing the stairs. "You'll still have math to finish," she said. "Got your breath mints?"

"Huh?" What was he packing? Oh, yeah. Socks.

CHAPTER 5

THE SECRET CELL OF SINISTERNESS

Meanwhile . . . Malevia Spleene hung the last of her counterfeit twenty-dollar bills to dry in the warehouse she jokingly called her money laundry and rode home on a bicycle she'd stolen from a starving orphan. She dumped the bike where a bus would be sure to run over it, then ran into the house and up to the Secret Cell of Sinisterness, also known as her room.

"Dinner's almost ready," her dad called as she thumped up the stairs.

Malevia shut her door. On her laptop, she scrolled to a video loop of Arizona desert. She projected it on the screen she'd set up in front of her shelf of evil female action figures. She turned on all the lights and put on sunglasses. Then she clicked through the video links on her tablet. The last one was not connected. Malevia muttered something nasty. She should have known: "call NOW," the text had read, but The Boss always kept her waiting.

Malevia had picked arch-villain for her career back in grade two, when she watched *The Wizard of Oz* and liked the Wicked Witch better than Dorothy and Toto (especially Toto). Even then she was smart enough not to tell anyone. When people asked her what she wanted to be, she had always said astronaut or veterinarian, though she loathed heights and small animals. She didn't tell anyone *that* either. Her parents, who ran Hot Diggity Dog, a charity for legless dachshunds, wouldn't have understood.

Now she was fifteen, a certified genius with a brand new Ph.D. in artificial intelligence, and ready to get started. Malevia had a long list of role models: Ursula, the Black Widow, various fairy tale queens and, of course, Cruella de Vil. But costumes, equipment, minions and snacks didn't grow on trees. You needed start-up money. Arch-villainy wasn't the kind of business you could get a bank loan for. You could *rob* a bank, but that was petty crime. Malevia liked to think big.

Right now she had an "unpaid" gig as an intern for a master criminal known only as The Boss. Malevia had found ways to cheat on the "unpaid" part. She hadn't stolen enough to quit yet, so it was still important to keep The Boss happy, at least until she found out who The Boss was.

A cheesy ring tone sounded on her tablet. On-screen an image popped up: a head and shoulders in a cheap Darth Vader costume. The Boss wore a different disguise every time, each one lamer than the last.

"Spleene! What took so long?" It was a woman's voice, Malevia was sure, not much more than a smoky whisper.

"Sorry." Malevia made sure to pant. She fanned herself. "It was hard to get a signal out here."

"Where are you?"

"The Grand Canyon. I thought it might be a good place to stash gold bullion."

"I'll do the thinking around here, Spleene. You dropped the ball on Lundborg."

"Lundborg? What are you talking about? I tailed him to the hospital, watched all day. Plus I had someone in the lab on my payroll. All the tests were negative. The kid is a washout. He can't tie his shoes without tripping on the laces."

The whisper turned venomous. "You didn't wait long enough. They retested that night. He has a power.

I want it. And him. I went to Dimly myself, but he's *gone*, Spleene. Vanished. *And it's your bad."*

"I'll find him," Malevia said instantly. "Kidnapping? You got it. Torture? My pleasure. Murder? On special this week."

"Don't be an idiot. You're off this assignment. You're going to Pianvia instead. I have a mining project there that needs taking care of."

"Pianvia? But—"

"Suck it up, Spleene. You're off to the worst start of any intern I've ever had. You're just lucky I had other reasons to go to Dimly. If you mess up in Pianvia, you'll lose more than your job."

"You're already not paying me."

"I know how you're cheating me on the elevator hijacks and plastic sushi. They're the only things you've done that impress me. You can lose more than money, Spleene. Your head, for instance."

Malevia considered this. "I hear Pianvia is nice in the spring."

"I agree. I may come to see for myself. All you need to know now is that we'll need to hijack a trainload of garlic there. Soon. I'll send details. Get going and start planning."

"I'll need money for travel."

"Take it out of what you've skimmed from the cat

racing. I know about that too." The screen went blank.

Malevia sighed and shut down the link. She chose a passport from her collection and booked a flight to Pianvia. She had an entire football team of animatronic Green Bay Packer bots in storage. Malevia had built them for a failed attempt to rig the Super Bowl, back when she was twelve. They'd be handy for a train heist. How many would she need? She'd have to do a web search on train hijacking.

She also had to plan maximum payback for a certain double-crossing lab mouse — another reason to loathe small animals. At least she'd paid with counterfeit cheddar. As for Lundborg (What kind of power could a klutz like him have?), he wasn't her problem anymore.

"Dinner," called her mom.

Malevia joined her parents on the backyard patio. "Guess what?" she gushed. "I've been invited to Mexico for three weeks. We're starting a non-profit hostel for migrating butterflies."

"Wonderful," chorused her parents. The legless dachshunds around them wagged their tails. Malevia promised herself to kick one before she left.

CHAPTER 6

ROLLING IN CASHEWS

The Boss killed the Skype link and turned. A mouse lounged behind her, impeccably dressed for summer business in a bespoke white linen suit over a T-shirt of pale blue silk, and hand-woven loafers of buttery leather. Empty peanut shells were scattered around him.

"Malevia has a lot to learn," said The Boss. "You were right to come straight to me. I like a take-charge mouse."

"And I like a good disguise," Claude said, picking his teeth with a staple.

"We're well matched. There's room in this organization for a go-getter. Find Lundborg for me again. Don't harm him. He could be even more useful than the others."

Claude nodded. He dropped the staple, stood and brushed a peanut crumb from his suit, then picked up a satchel that matched his shoes. "Done and done. I'll be in touch." He looked around for cats, hopped down from the desk, and hurried to the door.

"Soon," The Boss called after him. "Sooner than soon. And keep your receipts."

Claude's eyes narrowed. "From here on in, I'm not working for peanuts."

"Of course not," purred The Boss. "Find the boy — fast — and you'll be rolling in cash . . . ews," she finished, after Claude left. "Until my cats get hungry."

She sat thinking of all the evil she could wreak with Lundborg's telekinetic power, especially if combined with some of the others' gifts. Speaking of which, there was more messaging to do and fear to create. A fresh disguise was needed.

She picked one from the closet, then pulled off the Darth Vader mask and picked up her perfume spritzer. After all these years she still wasn't used to the smell of burnt rubber. In the mirror she saw nothing at all.

CHAPTER 7

WATCH OUT FOR TOWELS

A Toronto motorcycle cop was writing out parking tickets for The Boss's shabby brown blimp, which was tethered to six expired parking meters. Claude scampered down a mooring cable and hopped into the cop's saddlebag. Police were good to catch rides with because they never obeyed the speed limit.

On the way downtown, he took off his business clothes and stowed them carefully in his satchel. In the wider world it was best to look as inconspicuous as possible. Besides, his duds had cost a bomb, and they weren't easy to keep clean — or replace. He had to order everything from a maker of doll clothes in Nova Scotia, who took forever. Then he poked his nose out of the saddlebag. Fresh air was a relief after the combined stench of burnt rubber and cats in that blimp.

Not long after, satchel slung over his shoulder and clutching the last of the cop's bagel, he scooted onto a bus at the terminal and made himself comfy under a back seat. He had an idea where that skinflint Cheeper had taken Gary, but he needed to be sure.

Claude's new life as a freelance mastermind was going pretty well. It had been a no-brainer to double-cross Malevia Spleene about Lundborg. (As if he couldn't tell fake cheddar! Who did she think she was dealing with?) Granted, the trip to Dimly had been a pain: Lundborg's cat had almost killed him. Plus he'd almost drowned in a disgusting puddle of slime near that other kid Flem's place. Dimly was a dump, Claude thought, and Lundborg was a doofus. But now he had the chance of a lifetime. This could pay off bigger than reality TV.

He left the bus at a crossroads stop two hours north and hopped onto a pickup truck at the traffic light. A kilometre farther, at the sign for Camp Pan-American, he hopped off and hurried through the gate. Cheeper had brought the lab crew here last fall to plan a superpower training centre hidden inside this regular summer camp.

Claude had not been impressed: dial-up internet, bad food, boring country air instead of exotic city smells, and the local mice were hicks who spoke with accents. One scurried by him now as he started up the driveway.

"Watch out for towels," it muttered, then vanished in the weeds. Claude shrugged and pressed on. Who knew hicks were clean freaks?

Through the twilight, he could hear the grating sounds of a school group having fun. Claude sped toward a light glowing in the window of the farthest cabin. Scrambling up a downspout, he peeked inside. Sure enough, there were Lundborg, Cheeper, Sergeant Stan Muldoon and others Claude didn't know.

Lundborg was saying, "Sorry about the zip line thing, again. Maybe I ate too much garlic." *He's right about that*, Claude thought. He could smell the kid's breath from outside.

"Not a problem, Gary," Cheeper said. His voice sounded as if it was. Claude noticed Cheeper had a cast on one arm and a black eye. "We all learned from it. You probably won't use a zip line anyway, at least not in the dark."

Lundborg nodded. "I really do better with Kirsten around. You'll see."

"I called your parents. She'll join you in a couple of days, but we're going now. Are you packed? We've got a flight to catch."

Claude's ears pricked up. He'd gotten here just in time. The Boss would love him for this. Could he cut a reality TV deal too? Talking mice, a telekinetic fumbler and a tacky villain trying to take over the world: Who could resist? It would be bigger than *The Bachelor.* Claude smelled limos and Limburger replacing blimps and bagels. Soon it would be suits all the time.

He had to find out where they were going, and then get out of here. What would be the best way? Claude saw Cheeper was wearing immense cargo shorts. He'd bet there was a phone in one of those pockets, and lots of room in the others. Cheeper would never even notice Claude was along for the ride. Should he gnaw through the screen or slip under the door?

Claude's whiskers tingled. The air pulsed and he dove for the grass an instant before death could snatch him. Something circled and swooped again. Claude scrambled for the downspout as talons tore off his satchel. He dove into the opening. Overhead, a beak viciously raked the metal.

Panting, he cursed. That hick mouse had been talking about the *owls*, not towels. Outside he heard rustling as the bird settled in to wait. Then came the sounds of voices, slamming doors and a vehicle starting up and pulling away. Claude cursed again.

He'd never found out where they were going. And his clothes were gone. Next came a faint drumming noise. Claude felt a cold trickle beneath his tail: it had started to rain.

Reality TV was on hold. When he got out of here, there was only one message he could send, to The Boss: *Follow the sister.*

CHAPTER 8

EGGS-ITEMENT

"Oh, wow," Gary breathed, "this is for us?"

It was midnight. He was standing under the lights at an air force base, with Cheeper and Sergeant Stan Muldoon. A C5M Super Galaxy transport plane was warming up on the tarmac.

"Well, we're hitching a ride on it," grinned Muldoon as a stream of trucks drove up a ramp and into the plane's belly. Just what Muldoon was a sergeant in had not been made clear at training. All Gary knew was, the sergeant was the most cheerful person he'd ever met, upbeat even when Gary had accidentally levitated the raccoons.

"Better than paying for it," said Cheeper. "Imagine the fuel bill." He turned to Gary and Muldoon.

"Gentlemen, this is where I leave you. The CIA will be waiting to rendezvous. Good luck, and keep all your receipts." He shook hands with them, awkwardly because of the cast, then limped back into the hangar.

"C'mon, Gary," said Sergeant Muldoon. They shouldered their backpacks and walked up the ramp. Inside the plane was like a warehouse. Their footsteps echoed past vehicles, rows of shipping containers, stacks of skids and shelving units, to an area crammed with farm machinery, hay bales, cages and pens with barnyard animals.

"I hear they're setting up a model farm in Blatistan," Muldoon said. "But c'mon. You're going to like this." He led Gary around a bulkhead. Seats stretched along one side of a passenger area. The rest of the space was taken up by a small, computerized driving range, exercise machines and a basketball half court. A roller cart of basketballs sat under the backboard.

"This is your chance," said Muldoon. He checked his watch. "We'll be mid-flight when your power kicks in."

The plane was noisy and the seats uncomfortable. Gary didn't care. He stoked up on garlic pasta and waited impatiently. The instant he could levitate his seat tray he hit the basketball court. He'd been looking forward to this a long time.

Standing at the foul line, Gary polished his glasses, wiped his hands on his jersey, and shoved his bangs up under his tuque. He looked at the basketballs. He thought one off the cart and into his hands. It came in like a perfect chest pass. Gary tried a foul shot. It began to fall short. Gary thought fast. The ball looped back up and plopped through the net. Basket.

Oh.

Yeah.

He ran for the ball, tripped on a shoelace, then lofted a wonky jumper from the baseline. It banged high off the rim. Falling, he thought-jammed it back down through the hoop. Basket. Telekinetic hook shot from the key: basket. Telekinetic three-pointer, left hand: basket. Right hand: basket. Double-pump fake to a layup: he tripped on his laces again, but thought the ball in anyway. Basket.

"Amazing," said Sergeant Muldoon, putting down his book.

"Twenty-one?" offered Gary as picked himself up. He so wished Kirsten were here.

"Now you're talking," Muldoon winked. "Loser does KP first night in camp."

"Huh?"

Gary didn't miss a shot in six straight games. Muldoon didn't seem to mind losing. "Fantastic,

Gary. You are so going to rock this mission."

"I'll be shooting baskets?"

"No, but you've got the eye and touch we need. I knew you would; absolutely golden. And that concentration, whoo boy! Lovin' it. Now that I've got all the KP I can handle I'm going to take a little break. You might want to do the same." He walked to his seat and picked up his book. It was called *Be the Bright Side.*

For the first time since he'd started Clumsborging, Gary felt a glow of confidence. He was going to rock the mission with his superpower. Oh yeah, times two. He shot a few more telekinetic hoops then thought the ball back onto the cart. It was time for a new challenge.

He went to the golf area. There was a platform to hit from and a computerized screen to aim at, to show where your shot would have landed. Gary's dad had taken him to a place like this near Winnipeg.

Gary took a club from the rack. The big screen showed a picture of a fairway. He flipped the *Start* switch on the golf-ball dispenser. A ball popped out. He swung and missed. Another ball popped out. By his seventh shot he could think the ball anywhere he wanted it to go. It didn't matter that the video play-back showed his swing was somewhere between a slapshot and a bunt.

Another ball popped out, and another. Gary ignored them. He was already so good it was boring. He'd never thought *that* would happen.

What else was there to do? He wandered to the farm shipment. It was familiar stuff; Gary's grandparents had a farm just outside Dimly. The animals were restless in the plane. A rooster crowed and Gary remembered something he'd always wanted to do.

He found the chicken coop and peered in. Just as he'd hoped. He thought out five eggs and landed them on a nearby console labelled *Loading Control*. He thought one egg into the air, then two, then three. They hovered before him. He concentrated hard. The eggs began to rotate like a Ferris wheel. His hands

flapped, helping them along. Something bumped at his foot. Gary didn't break concentration.

He felt for the fourth egg and lobbed it into the middle, working the egg into the rotation. Oh yeah, times four. Wait till he showed Sergeant Muldoon.

"Sergeant Muldoon," he called. "Look!"

Another bump. Gary ignored it. He felt for the fifth egg. There were more bumps to each foot. "SERRR-GEANNNT!"

"Coming." He heard Muldoon's voice, then "*WHOAA—*" and a *thump.* Gary jumped. His feet landed in a river of golf balls that shot out from under him. He pitched forward onto the egg and a large red button on the console.

An alarm blared and all the pens opened at once. The animals thundered out, then toppled like bowling pins, sliding into a maelstrom of bleats and squeals that drowned out the alarm. There was a blizzard of straw, then the animals were up and scattering. Gary sprawled over the console, gasping. Something was lapping at his hand: a dog was licking the broken egg. Goats were slurping up golf balls. Tails swishing, a pony and some cows vanished into the maze of shipping containers.

Sergeant Muldoon crawled around the bulkhead in a stream of more balls. Over the blaring of the alarm he called, "Gary, what's going on?" A pig rumbled past him, going the other way.

Gary pushed his hat up with his dry hand. "Huh?"

It took to the very last of Gary's power and an hour's regular work after that for them to set things back to rights. Even then, there were still a couple of chickens perched out of reach and a donkey that wouldn't come out of an armoured personnel carrier.

Gary slumped in his seat, crushed. So much for his perfect touch. So much for whoo-boy concentration. This had been his worst Clumsborging ever. He had a feeling that if Kirsten didn't arrive in time, the mission was doomed.

"Um, like, sorry. Again," he said to Sergeant Muldoon.

"Gary, every problem is an opportunity," said Muldoon. "That's the way I look at it." Something squealed beneath his seat. Gary leaned down and pulled out a piglet. "We've learned from this," said Muldoon, taking it and scratching behind its ears.

"Like what?" Gary asked sourly.

"Well, that sheep like *Be the Bright Side.*" Muldoon nodded at the chewed cover of his book. "And that we should be aware of our limits. *And* that we can use your power to bounce back. Look at how you rounded up those golf balls for us! Mighty impressive.

I've got nothing but positives from this."

He also had straw in his hair and goose poop on his boots, but Gary didn't go there. There was an important question to ask and he needed to work up to it. "So, how long till . . ."

"We arrive?" Muldoon checked his watch. "With plane changes, layovers, the chopper ride in . . ." He hoisted an eyebrow, calculating, "All told, say twenty hours."

"Where are we going again?"

"Pianvia, Gary. A little country in the Balkans. Very few people go there. We talked about it, remember? The CIA is waiting and base camp is ready."

Gary didn't remember. This did not help him feel better. To make up for forgetting he said, "There's a Pianvia Pancake Party every winter in Dimly. They wear funny hats. That look like pancakes. And you eat them. Pancakes, I mean."

Muldoon nodded. "I'm not surprised. I remember reading that some Pianvians settled on the Prairies. Do you know any?"

"Huh?" Gary had no idea. He moved on to a more important question: "Do I start as soon as we get there?"

"We'll show you the set-up Day One and then you're good to go."

Gary got to the question he *really* wanted to ask: "Will Kirsten get there before I start?"

"That's the plan. But even if she doesn't, I know you can do it on your own."

"On *my own*?"

"You've got what it takes, buddy. You'll rock it either way. But don't worry about that right now. I'm sure Kirsten will make it in time. Now, get some shut-eye. We've got a long way to go."

Gary sank back and pulled his hat down over his eyes. His hand was still sticky from the egg. He gave it a little wipe on the hat. If Sergeant Muldoon expected him to do whatever he had to do on his own, they had an even longer way to go. Before Gary could think anymore, he was asleep.

CHAPTER 9

WHAT GOES UP

The helicopter came in low, under the radar. In the morning light Gary saw they were skimming over a vast oatmeal swamp that reminded him of that odd puddle back in Dimly, not to mention a difficult part of his *Gang of Greats* game.

The chopper set down in the foothills beyond. Mountains loomed. Gary stumbled out under the whirling blades, following Sergeant Muldoon. As the chopper rose in a blast of downdraft, a rider emerged from the shelter of some scrubby trees. He was on something like a small buffalo and leading two more with colourful saddles and harnesses.

"Tapioca," Sergeant Muldoon called. "Hi, Tex."

"Howdy, Stan. Welcome to Pianvia." Tex wore a

poncho with bright stripes and a flat hat that drooped alarmingly, like a large and soggy pancake. Gary thought again of the winter party in Dimly.

"Gary, this is Tex. He's CIA, base and mission commander." Muldoon made introductions. "Tex, Gary. Gary is our secret weapon."

"Pleasure," Tex nodded. He dug ponchos and hats out of saddlebags. "Put 'em on, boys. Look local, we're here undercover. Then mount up and we'll head to base. I'll brief you as we go."

Gary and Muldoon pulled on the clothes. Gary straightened his glasses and saw that the hat made Muldoon look like a demented mushroom. That probably meant he did too, especially since he'd pulled the hat on over his regular one.

"Haven't ridden a yak for ages," said Muldoon, swinging into the saddle. "Love 'em."

Gary scrambled aboard his own on the third try. He held on tight.

"Let's ride," said Tex. Gary's yak loped in behind. Muldoon rode beside him. "Here's the picture," Tex said over his shoulder. "See that mountain ahead?"

It was hard to miss. The mountain's sheer face was scarred by a road that zigzagged to the summit. Gary made out a cluster of buildings at the top.

"That mountain was full of reidium," Tex said.

"Down below was mined out years ago, so they built a road to the top and started again up there. When the market for reidium dried up because the stuff was so dangerous, the Pianvians abandoned the mine. Now our satellites show somebody's working up there and they've turned it into a fortress."

"If it isn't the Pianvians, who is it?" asked Muldoon.

"Good question. Our drone surveillance shows a combination of moles and the Green Bay Packers. The moles do the grunt work, the actual mining."

Muldoon's eyebrows bunched. "You mean real moles? Little furry guys, weak eyes, live underground?"

"Hey," Tex said, "why not? It's a mountain of reidium, and Pianvia's main crop is garlic. If Dr. F. can get super mice out of the combo, who's to say you won't get super moles occurring naturally here? The Packers are doing security."

"The NFL Green Bay Packers? The actual team?"

"Nah," Tex said. "Probably Pianvian thugs. This country is cut off from the world. They're crazy for any kind of Western clothes here."

"But who's in charge?" Muldoon pressed.

"So far, we've only got one person." Tex pulled a phone from under his poncho, punched up a photo on the screen, and handed it back. The grainy image showed a teenage girl with a blond ponytail. "Malevia Spleene," Tex said, "a nasty one. She's on security watch lists worldwide. Word is she almost rigged the Super Bowl a few years back."

Muldoon whistled. Tex went on, "Our intercepts turn up traffic to 'The Boss,' so there's somebody higher up. We don't know who. All we know is, this Boss is always on the move. And wants reidium, big time."

Tex turned to face them. "Anyone with enough garlic and enough guts can refine reidium. And any bad dude with refined reidium is a threat to the world, especially now that we know about its, uh, *extra* power." He nodded at Gary. "This mining operation has to be stopped. Gary's the key."

"He can do it!" smiled Muldoon.

Gary remembered the inflight stampede. He wished he was back in Dimly. "Can I get home in time for basketball camp?" This came out more squeak than speech but Tex smiled as he took his phone back. "I like a can-do attitude. Welcome aboard, pardner."

"Why not just call in a missile strike?" Muldoon asked. *Yessss,* thought Gary, *Pleeease. Problem solved.*

Tex said, "We will, but first we want the reidium they've mined. That stuff is hard to come by. Imagine what Dr. F. could do with a big supply, instead of scrounging a few grains from old light bulbs."

"I get you," said Muldoon. Gary didn't.

Tex went on, "The reidium's all up there, waiting for transport. We're going to steal it from them before they can move it. That's where Gary comes in." Tex squinted at Gary. "You can really do this tele-stuff?"

Gary's yak farted.

"Can he ever!" Muldoon chimed in. He looked at his watch. "It's almost nine o'clock. We're six hours ahead of Montreal here, so this is prime time. Go for it, Gary."

Gary sighed. He shoved back his pancake hat and looked around. What would be easy and impress

Tex? Up the hill lay a pile of rocks. He got one of his feelings.

"See those?" Gary thought a small rock into the air. It wobbled and hung there. Tex whistled. Gary made the rock swing gently back and forth.

"Amazing," Tex said.

"Isn't that fantastic?" said Muldoon. "Good stuff, Gary."

The rock was getting heavy. Gary let go. As he did, he got another one of his feelings — this time like the one he'd had skateboarding. Again it was too late. The rock crashed onto the pile, which shuddered and began to rumble toward them.

"Avalanche!" cried Muldoon. The ground shook. The yaks wheeled and plunged. Gary slammed into his yak's neck, getting a mouthful of fur. He held on with his teeth.

The rumbling faded to a series of plops as the rocks hit the swamp. The yaks calmed. Gary sat up. His face and glasses were greasy with whatever oil was in yak fur. His pancake hat lay on the ground nearby. He thought it up as far as his yak's head and left it there. The yak didn't seem to mind.

Muldoon trotted his yak over, chuckling. "You know the old saying, what goes up must come down." He slapped Gary on the back. "Get a load of the power this dude can unleash, Tex! We're talking awesome."

The slap made Gary burp up some yak fur he'd swallowed.

"Hmm," Tex said. "The plan may need a little fine tuning."

CHAPTER 10

WHAT BLOWS UP

Base camp was a yak herder's hut at the foot of the mountain. The air was fresher here. Gary was glad; his ride had been making him seasick. He struggled from the saddle and rubbed his aching backside.

Between camp and mountain was a meadow dotted with grazing yaks. In the distance lay a dirt road and a railway track. They unsaddled their mounts and turned them loose. Tex led Gary and Muldoon to the hut. Inside were crude bunks, a wood stove and a rickety table with an oil lamp. Tex pushed the stove aside and lifted a trap door. They climbed down a ladder to a snug bunker outfitted with generators and computer equipment.

"One yak in the pasture is a fake," Tex said,

powering up a laptop. "That's where Gary will work from. It's positioned close to the mountain to link with communications and surveillance. We've got drones in the air twenty-four seven."

The men looked at him. "I'll do way better when my sister gets here," Gary offered. He settled his bent glasses on his nose. "Really."

"Good to know," Tex said. He handed round freeze-dried army rations and garlic pills for Gary. Now that his seasickness had passed, Gary found he was starving. As they ate, Tex angled the laptop screen toward them and clicked through a photo file, explaining what had to be done.

"It's simple, really. The reidium is kept in these storage bins in the middle of the compound." A picture showed two blue plastic containers like the one the Lundborgs stored their skates in.

"That's not very much," said Muldoon.

"Doesn't matter," Tex said. "A few grams of reidium, refined, could convert the electrical charge from an orange into enough power to light New York City for a year — or blow it to smithereens. The same few grams could create dangerous superpowers in who knows what. With those two bins you could rule the world. Or destroy it." Tex clicked to the next pictures.

"The moles bring the stuff to the surface in toy dump trucks. They pack it in numbered pencil cases. The loaded cases are light enough for them to carry up those little ramps into the storage tubs." The pictures showed a pile of bulging cases, each printed with a picture of a chubby cat grinning and waving a paw.

"Five days from now an express freight carrying fifteen tonnes of Pianvian garlic will pass along that railway track. Our intel says the Packers are going to hijack the train, load the reidium and as much garlic as they can on two old school buses they've got up there, then make a run for it across the border to Dystopia.

"Now, Spleene's a teenager, so she's nocturnal. Moles aren't, but she's got them working night shifts only, to suit her schedule, apparently by giving them all the earthworms they can eat. She and the moles sleep all day. The guards have limited vision because of their football helmets. So here's the plan: For the next two mornings, when nobody's noticing, we use Gary's power to secretly swap those reidium-filled pencil cases for these—" Tex opened a box at his feet, filled with identical, but empty, pencil cases, "—which we'll pack with harmless dirt. We get the reidium, they get garlic and dirt. Best part is, they'll never know what happened. They'll just think the mine has run out of reidium, so they won't come back. And that way they'll never find out that we flattened the mine with a missile strike after they left, so it can never be used again. With any luck, they'll take us to this Boss instead. Like it?"

Gary found himself nodding along with Muldoon. It seemed like a pretty cool plan. "What exactly do I have to do again?" he asked.

"I'll show you tomorrow," Tex said. He looked hard at Gary. "Unrefined reidium is explosive as all get-out. Can you handle this?"

"I think so. 'Cause Kirsten will be here. She's coming tomorrow, right?"

Tex looked at Muldoon. "Gary," Sergeant Muldoon said gently, "I got a message. Kirsten's been delayed.

Apparently she has a big soccer game she doesn't want to miss. We have to start before she gets here."

"What? We can't start without Kirsten. She helps me concentrate." Gary's thoughts swirled; so did all the food packets. Noodles and freeze-dried ice cream hit the laptop and *Be the Bright Side*. "Sorry."

"It's okay, Gary. Calm down. Know what will help us even more? Taking it easy today. Our body clocks are out of whack from travelling. We'll rest up now, have a little practice later and just take it as it comes tomorrow. No pressure. Problems are opportunities, remember?" Sergeant Muldoon wiped off his book.

Gary nodded. He *was* tired.

"And I'm on KP," said Muldoon, "thanks to a certain can't-miss basketball dude. And the way you spun that rock today? You're still the man, Gare. Listen, why not get outside and chill? Soak up some rays. You could scoop a little dirt into some of these pencil cases. Just keep your hat on. We don't want anyone up there seeing our faces."

Ten minutes later Gary sat drowsing behind the hut. He'd started scooping dirt into cases, but his mind was already drifting. The sun was warm, and unlike Dimly, there were no mosquitoes. What had he been thinking about? Oh yeah, *Gang of Greats*, and Life Extensions. Jess Flem was already an Elfling named Firefly or Ferriswheel or something. Gary was still a Troll who fell into swamps.

He remembered the swamp today. Which reminded him of the puddle back in Dimly. Which reminded him of missing the school trip to the Winnipeg Flood Museum. Which reminded him of missing all those layups on the school basketball team. Which reminded him of all the disasters since. Gary sagged against the wall of the hut. Voices murmured inside.

"We don't have time to wait for the sister, Stan, especially if he's only good for three hours a day. Gotta start tomorrow. Does his breath always smell that bad?"

Sergeant Muldoon said something. Tex's voice came back again. ". . . risk we'll have to take . . ."

Murmur, murmur.

"Well, if he does, remember what you said about what goes up? It'll be what *blows* up instead. The whole place will blow sky high, and us with it. That would destroy the mine, so it would still count as a win. Wouldn't get us any medals, though. Then again, there wouldn't be enough of us left to pin medals on."

Gary started awake. Huh? What had he been thinking about? Oh yeah, Life Extensions.

CHAPTER 11

HOW TO RETRIEVE REIDIUM (IN CASE YOU WONDERED)

"There's nothing to it, Gary," Tex said the next morning. They were all in the meadow, beside the fake yak. The sun had not yet crested the mountain peak, and Gary was glad of his hats and poncho. Looking up, he saw the zigzag scar of the switchback road. Buzzards perched like black question marks. "Do it the way we ran through last night," Tex said.

Muldoon placed a pail beside him. It held pencil cases filled with dirt. Gary knelt beside the yak as if he was going to milk it. He yanked on the tail. A patch of pelt rolled up, revealing a screen at eye level. He tapped past a music video, a man in a chef's hat, a woman holding a crocodile and an infomercial for reclining chairs. A drone's-eye view of the mountaintop appeared.

Fencing and razor wire bordered the compound, patrolled by three burly guards in green-and-gold football uniforms. Just inside the gate sat two school buses, next to them a yak corral. In the middle of everything was a double-wide trailer bristling with satellite dishes and antennae. Across from it a ramshackle archway led into the mountain.

"Spleene's headquarters and the mine entrance," said Tex. "The shipping container over there is for the guards." Apart from the three on patrol the place looked deserted. "Everyone is snoozing," Tex said. "That means we're operational. Go for it, Gary."

Gary tapped the screen. There were the blue storage bins. Parked beside them was a line of toy dump trucks. *What came first? Oh yeah.*

He thought off one of the lids and fitted it onto the other. Now the screen showed the pencil cases in the bin, bulging with reidium ore. It was about half-full. He thought two cases out. For an instant he remembered the eggs. The cases wobbled.

"Concentrate," said Muldoon. "Keep 'em low. Change views."

Gary focused. The cases steadied. He touched the screen to a longer view, then whisked the cases across the compound, behind a guard, and levitated them over the fence.

"A-one, pardner," Tex breathed. "Change the view. Bring 'em down."

Gary touched the screen and began to think the pencil cases down the mountain. "Easy does it," Muldoon whispered. "Remember to breathe."

A buzzard flapped into the screen shot, snatched the cases out of the air, and sailed around an outcrop.

BOOM!

Black feathers wafted upward. More buzzards appeared, flapping toward them.

"Dang," Tex said. "At least they won't bother us for a while. They'll be too busy eating whatever's left of their buddy. Let's try it again."

"Okay. Just a sec," Gary said.

To his surprise, Gary felt calm. Maybe he could handle this after all. His hats were getting in the way though. He tugged them both back and down over his ears. This also anchored his glasses. His elbow bumped Tex, who was resetting the screen. A new picture popped up. It was a beach: gulls and logs, with ships in the background. In the middle of the picture was an amazingly tidy boy. Where had Gary seen him before? The boy was holding up a Chompo chocolate bar and saying something the hats blocked out.

"What's going on?" Gary asked. No answer. He looked at Tex and Muldoon. They were staring at the screen. "You guys?" Gary said. "Hey." No answer. He yanked the hats off his ears as the video ended.

"I had one with me," Muldoon was saying.

"We could order some," Tex said. "If I get a message out right now they could probably fly a few in tomorrow with Kirsten. C'mon, let's do it."

"Gotta be Chompo, though," Muldoon said. "I'll check my kit while we're at it. Gary, you hold the fort. Just wait for us. We'll be back in a jiff."

CHAPTER 12

MR. CONCENTRATION

Huh? Gary watched Tex and Muldoon hustle off across the pasture. What were they talking about? Gary looked at the screen. A stout man was giving a banjo lesson. He tapped back to the view of the mountaintop.

He could do more than hold the fort. If he could do this on his own it would make up for his mistakes so far. He thought about the avalanche and Mr. Cheeper's arm and . . . what else was there? Well, lots of things. That would all be forgotten. And he'd be a hero — a superhero, in fact.

First he needed to get comfortable. Gary took the dirt-filled pencil cases from the bucket and piled them in the grass. He turned the bucket upside down, put his hat on it, and sat down. That was better. He thought over the best order to do things. Should he start by sending two cases up to replace the ones he'd taken? No, best to bring the reidium-filled ones down first. That was the important part — and that way he wouldn't mix them up.

Gary began bringing reidium down the mountain. He carefully laid the reidium cases beside the dirt-filled ones. To make sure he didn't get confused, he used a simple plan: *r*eidium to the *r*ight.

By the time he had the mountaintop bin emptied, Tex and Sergeant Muldoon still hadn't returned. Gary was tired and cold. The sun had reached the far side of his fake yak. He rose stiffly, moved the bucket into the sunshine, then turned the yak around on its rollers so he could still see the screen.

After a moment's stretching he got back to work. Now Gary was facing the two piles of pencil cases, which made the next part even easier. *R*eidium to the *r*ight, he reminded himself. Two by two he sent the left pile of pencil cases up the mountain, settled them snugly in the bin, and thought the lid back on.

Gary shut down the touch screen and yanked on the yak tail. The pelt rolled back down. How long had the job taken? Not that he was done. He turned over the bucket and began thinking a pencil case into it. A few centimetres up, it fell. The world stopped.

When it started again, the first thing Gary thought was, he was still alive. The second thing he thought was, it was lucky he hadn't lifted the case any higher. The third thing he thought was, his power time must be almost up.

When he stopped trembling he gently lifted the pencil cases into the bucket by hand and started back to the hut. He began to feel better again. This had to be the longest he'd concentrated in his life. Wait till he showed Tex and Muldoon. Wait till he told Kirsten. He imagined her watching him work his magic the next day and grinned. It was too bad she was coming all this way for nothing.

Tex and Muldoon came outside as he arrived. Muldoon was scratching his head. "You know, usually I don't even like chocolate bars."

"Well, we're stuck with them now," Tex said. Then, "Gary!"

"Today's mission accomplished. Ours are up, theirs are here. We're halfway done." Gary held up the bucket and promptly stumbled.

Tex snatched the bucket from him. "Easy there, pardner. Let me just take that and store it away."

"Fantastic, Gary. Great work." Muldoon clapped him on the back. Gary shrugged modestly, though he thought so too.

Right now he could do with a Chompo bar himself and, if he could get an internet connection later, a round of *Gang of Greats*. Now that he was Mr. Concentration he'd wipe Jess Firefly off the map, even with logs for thumbs. Then he'd message home saying how much fun camp was.

CHAPTER 13

SPLORG VINU GROZNAB

After lunch they all sat outside, cleaning their yak harnesses. Even with mints, Gary's breath was easier to take outside. They'd already filled another pile of pencil cases with dirt. *Gang of Greats* would happen later; Gary had forgotten the time difference between Pianvia and Canada. In Dimly it was about seven o'clock in the morning. Not even Jess Flem would be at her computer now.

"I'll meet Kirsten's chopper first thing in the morning." Tex went over their plans. "Gary, if Kirsten helps you stay focused, do you think we can finish tomorrow?"

Before Gary could answer, Muldoon murmured, "We've got company."

Gary peeked from under his hat. A hefty figure on a yak was loping across the pasture toward them. Whoever it was wore the Pianvian outfit of poncho and pancake hat, but it fit oddly. As the rider drew closer Gary realized this was because the hat sat atop a football helmet and the poncho was being worn over what had to be shoulder pads. Green and gold flashed below.

Tex and Muldoon tugged at their own ponchos. Underneath, Gary glimpsed pistols. "Don't react," said Tex. "Just watch him. And don't smile. They ain't huggers, to put it mildly."

The rider stopped some metres off. Gary sensed that even without the football pads he'd be a big man. The hat and helmet made it impossible to see his face.

No one spoke. Tex and Muldoon kept at their work. Gary tried to do the same. The rider swung stiffly from his mount, reached into his saddlebag, and placed something on the ground. Then, just as stiffly, he climbed back on his yak and rode back toward the mountain.

When he was gone they walked to what he'd left behind: a human skull, perched on a squat brown bottle.

"What's this about?" asked Muldoon.

"If I'm not mistaken," Tex replied, "I think we've just been challenged to a game of fleever."

"Fleever?"

"It's the national sport. It's kind of like polo, except you ride yaks and the ball is the skull of a vanquished enemy. C'mon inside, I'll show you."

In the hut Tex flipped through his copy of *Pianvia for Dummies.* A photo showed a crowd of riders on wheeling yaks. The players were swinging mallets at something in the grass.

"From two to ten players on a team," Tex read out. "The game is won by the first team to score three goals. Winners get the yaks, or the right to chop off the losers' heads. A challenge is delivered by placing a skull on an empty Splotnik bottle. Games are always played in the morning."

Gary looked at the bottle. It had an unfamiliar yellow and red label.

"Do they have that stuff at the Dimly pancake wing-ding?" asked Muldoon.

Gary shrugged. "Huh? Is it like maple syrup?"

"Nope," said Tex. "Splotnik is the Pianvian national drink. It's eighty percent alcohol, made from fermented pork rinds."

Gary uncorked the bottle. The smell that came out was hair-raising, even without telekinesis. He coughed and held it at arm's length. Words had been scratched into the glass above the label. *"Splorg vinu groznab,"* he read out slowly.

Muldoon turned pages. "Nothing in 'Commonly Used Phrases,'" he shrugged.

"Never mind that," said Tex. "This changes everything. The game will be right when Gary is supposed to be swapping cases."

"What if Gary worked through the game?" asked Muldoon. "They'd all be distracted."

Tex shook his head. "No can do. To get the video feed, the fake yak has to be right smack where we'll be playing. And they'll expect Gary to play; Kirsten too, for that matter. Only thing to do is win the game, and quick, before Gary's power expires. So here's the roundup: I meet Kirsten's chopper first thing. Don't come out or start the game until we get back. You're going to have to work double quick tomorrow, Gary. And they might be more active up there. I'm darn grateful you did so much today. Without it, we'd be busted, buckaroos."

"With Kirsten here, no problem," Muldoon put in. "Right, Gary? Guaranteed to keep you cucumber cool."

"Huh? Oh yeah." Especially now that he knew you could Clumsborg a pencil case a little bit. That took some pressure off. Gary had a more important question. "So if we lose, will they chop our heads off?"

Muldoon shook his head. "Nah, that's old school. Any Pianvian wearing an NFL uniform is going to think modern, so torture at most." He grinned. "Don't worry, Gary. We've got this. Tex and I are good riders. If that guy's buddies are as big as him, their yaks will be slow as molasses. Besides, we have a secret weapon, don't we?"

"Huh? What is it?"

"You," said Tex.

CHAPTER 14

FLEEVER ACHIEVER

Tex left before dawn to meet Kirsten's chopper. Down in the bunker, Gary went online. It was about an hour after midnight back home, prime time for gamers like Jess. Despite Muldoon's assurance that they'd win the fleever game, he was a little nervous. A round of *Gang of Greats* might take his mind off things.

It didn't. He was *that* close to a Life Token when the Gorg popped up from nowhere, swinging his flaming axe. AsseomeDud27 dodged, only to bounce off a TigerCat that had somehow escaped the Fortress of Fantastic. It reared, shredding a tree. Gary knew he didn't have enough power to kill it, but he tried to conjure a MongooseSter anyway. Instead, his flailing thumbs sent AsseomeDud27 careening into the Misty Swamp and well . . . *Geez*, Gary thought. Meanwhile, he could see Elfling Firebug, or whoever Jess was, breezing on. Gary gave up and sent out a message, his thumbs tripping a little: "Anuyone know wjat SPLORG VINU GROZNAB meeams?"

To Gary's surprise, a reply popped up a few minutes later: "From a friend means your nana has nice tomatoes. If a fleever ? challenge means rabid dogs will chew your severed head."

Gary stared at the answer for a long moment. It had been sent by Dandelionheart.

"Whho thiiis?" he typed.

"Daisy," came back the reply. "Wassup?"

Huh? An image of a girl in a Pianvian poncho popped into his head. Was this Jess's hippie friend? The one who'd moved? How could he even begin to tell her what was up? Before he could think of an answer, Muldoon was calling him from up in the hut. Gary climbed the ladder.

Peering out the window they watched ten hulking riders cross the yak pasture in the early morning light. Several herded the animals grazing there off to one side. "Good thing we moved the fake one last night," Muldoon said. It was behind the hut with the two they had ridden in on.

Other riders spread out. Some staked goal posts at either end of the pasture. One carried long-handled mallets to the centre of what was now a playing field; another held something white and round. "A skull," Muldoon murmured, looking through binoculars.

"What do we do?" Gary said.

"Sit tight. We wait for Tex and Kirsten. Look at these guys; they're so big their yaks can barely move. Easy pickings, Gary, especially with you."

Two hours later two riders approached from the west: Tex and Kirsten, in hats and ponchos. By now the Pianvians were lined up across the middle of the field, motionless on their yaks.

Gary and Muldoon stepped outside as Kirsten and Tex rode up. "Hey, Gare. Hi, Sergeant Muldoon," Kirsten greeted them. "I hear we've got a little riding game to play."

"Yeah, fleever," Gary said.

"Excellent! I haven't gone to riding camp three summers for nothing, you know." Kirsten patted her yak. "This little baby can go!"

"And look what I've got," Tex said to Muldoon. He lifted the flap on a saddlebag. Inside was a box of Chompo bars.

"You didn't have one yet?" said Muldoon.

"Waiting for you, pardner." Tex put Kirsten's

backpack and the box of chocolate bars inside the hut. "Let's get this done," he said. "We got business to attend to."

Everyone mounted their yaks and rode to midfield.

"Are they wearing football helmets?" Kirsten asked as they got closer.

"It's a fashion thing," Muldoon said.

"Weird."

"You don't know the half of it."

"Oh, yes I do. Tex told me."

At centre field they each took a mallet. Six of the opposing players rode to the sidelines, dismounted, and huddled away from their yaks. The remaining four players backed their mounts twenty paces. Gary's team did the same. The skull lay in the grass between them. Gary took a test swing with his mallet and almost hit his yak. *Clumsborg*, he thought.

Tex leaned over and whispered, "Leave the heavy lifting to me and Stan. We just need three goals and we need to get this done as fast as possible. If you do use your power, don't make it obvious. We can't give anything away."

A gunshot started the game. Both sides charged at the skull. Kirsten got there first. She whacked it sideways to Muldoon, then galloped her yak through a gap between two Pianvians. Muldoon shot her a forward pass, and Kirsten deftly knocked it downfield to Tex on the far side, who put it through the opposing goal as the other team struggled to catch up.

Gary, who hadn't gotten his own yak to move yet, jumped up in his stirrups to cheer. His yak started. Gary's glasses sailed off his nose. "Oh nooooo . . ." He was on hands and knees in the grass when the others returned and lined up again.

"What are you doing?" Kirsten called.

"Looking for my glass—"

The gunshot cracked. They galloped off. Gary kept searching. He couldn't be a secret weapon unless he could see.

Hooves thudded and the fleever game was a blurry tornado around him. He dove under his yak. With a *thok, thok, thok* of mallet on skull, the commotion faded, then came pounding back. Gary kept his eyes closed and hoped his yak wouldn't move. It was smelly down there, but safe.

The players roared off again. Gary sat up. His head bumped something. He looked and saw his glasses dangling in yak fur. Downfield, a cheer sounded.

He jammed his glasses on and scrambled back up. Muldoon, Kirsten and Tex were trading high-fives as they trotted back. Luckily they hadn't needed him so far. Now he saw that, behind his teammates, one of the Pianvians was carrying a different skull to centre field. *Huh?* Gary wondered if the first one had been wrecked by all that *thok*ing.

Kirsten and Tex were laughing, and Sergeant Muldoon was settling his hat as they rejoined Gary. "Back in business?" said Muldoon. "Two down, one to go."

"Huh?" Gary was looking downfield. The Pianvian players were carefully switching skulls. The rest of the Pianvians were backing up their yaks. No one else on his team noticed. *What was going on?*

"Hey—" he began.

The gunshot sounded. Kirsten, Tex and Muldoon sped for the skull. No one raced to meet them.

In the nick of time, Gary got one of his feelings. As Tex swung at the skull, Gary thought to it first and sent it spiralling at the Pianvians on the sidelines. One of them spun, faked left, and nabbed it with a diving, one-handed catch worthy of the real Green Bay Packers.

There was a blinding flash. A shockwave blew Gary's hats off. He never heard the explosion. A moment later padding, shoes, circuit boards and plastic limbs began to rain down, followed by scraps of ponchos and jerseys. A helmet bounced, sprouting a tangle of multicoloured wires and a camera lens.

Over where the Pianvians had been, nothing remained but a patch of scorched earth. The yaks had stampeded.

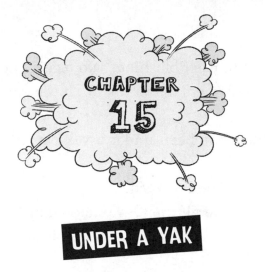

CHAPTER 15

UNDER A YAK

The buzzards swooped in, only to flap sadly away. What was left of the other team was riding off to the mountain.

Tex, Muldoon and Kirsten rode up beside him. "They were all bots," Muldoon marvelled.

"That'll be Spleene's doing." Tex nodded to Kirsten, "That was some mighty fine riding out there."

"No biggie," Kirsten shrugged.

Tex turned to Gary, "And I'm guessing I owe you majorly for saving my skin. That was you, sent it flying?"

Gary nodded. "I saw them switch skulls when you weren't looking."

"Thank you, pardner. I am much obliged — and mighty glad you found your glasses."

Gary felt himself blushing. "No biggie," he echoed Kirsten. "They were in the yak fur. It was weird down there."

"Anyone who's been under a yak can relate," said Muldoon.

"Have you?" said Kirsten.

"Uh-huh, several times." Muldoon didn't elaborate. Instead he said, "All it took was a bit of reidium in that skull."

Gary squinched his nose. "So how come the reidium didn't blow up yesterday?"

"It did," said Muldoon. "Remember the buzzard? I nearly had a heart attack when you stumbled with that pail."

"Yeah, but I dropped one of those cases and nothing happened."

"What?" Tex spun in his saddle. "C'mon." He turned and galloped his yak the rest of the way back. The others followed, Gary hanging on as best he could.

The cases were neatly packed in a blast-proof trunk hidden behind the hut. Muldoon unlocked it.

"What time is it?" Tex snapped. "You still got power?" In answer, Gary thought Kirsten's hat into the air. She giggled. Tex didn't. "All right, everybody down. Gary, send one of these far as you can, just like you did that skull."

Gary thought a pencil case into the air and sent it flying. They watched it plummet to the far side of the meadow. Nothing happened.

"See?" Gary said.

"Tell me exactly what you did yesterday," Tex said. "Step by step."

"Huh?"

"Good luck with that," said Kirsten.

Gary ignored her and thought back to the day before. It wasn't as hard as usual, because for once he had been concentrating. He told about emptying the bucket, bringing the reidium down, the two piles of pencil cases with *r*eidium to the *r*ight so he couldn't get mixed up, and sending the left pile back up the mountain.

"That's it?" Tex pressed. "Everything, Gary. Think hard."

"Oh. Yeah. Well, um, I got cold so I moved to the other side of the yak to be in the sun. I turned it around but I didn't change anything else, reidium to the right and everything."

Kirsten said gently, "But, Gare, if you turned around, that means the reidium wasn't on your right anymore. It was on your—"

"Left," Tex finished almost everyone's thought.

"Huh?" said Gary.

"Which means—" Tex went on, "you sent the reidium back up the mountain."

Muldoon groaned. "Which means we've got a pile of dirt." He unzipped a pencil case. "Except for this." He held up a breath mint. "We have to start all over."

"There isn't time," Tex said. "There was an intercept. The garlic train comes through tomorrow and they're going to move. And they may be on to us up there. We need a new plan, pronto."

CHAPTER 16

SOARING, BUZZARD STYLE

Meanwhile . . . Wearing hip waders and a parachute, Malevia Spleene watched from the mountain (well back from the edge) as half her offensive-team bots blew up. Lowering her binoculars, she cursed, then tapped commands onto her tablet to bring the remaining ones back.

What had gone wrong? She'd packed the reidium charge into that skull herself. How could that other fleever player have hit it back without setting off the explosion? It should have been the perfect way to get rid of whoever was down there. She cursed again. There was enough pressure already: the garlic train was arriving two days early and The Boss was arriving any minute.

Malevia didn't need this when she was so close to escaping the nightmare of Pianvia. If she'd known she would have to work with moles at dizzying heights she would never have come here, no matter how The Boss threatened her. Plus she'd had an overwhelming desire for a Chompo bar ever since she'd accidentally watched a weird internet video. She needed to get back home.

Instead she had to deal with *this*. The Boss wouldn't want witnesses, even local yokel yak herders. She guessed she'd just have to shoot them. Malevia raised her binoculars and peered through the swirl of buzzards to the pasture below. And froze. One of the Pianvians had taken off his hat. Except he wasn't a Pianvian, he was Gary Lundborg. She swept her gaze to the others. Two were men she didn't recognize. The third person turned, and Malevia recognized Lundborg's loathsome sister underneath the pancake headgear.

Malevia felt her spirits soar, buzzard-style. She thanked her dark stars she hadn't blown Lundborg up. The Boss would not have been pleased, to say the least.

Some scheming was needed to decide her next move. She had to make the choice of a lifetime. Should she hand Lundborg to The Boss as a surprise bonus?

That would make her reputation and raise her asking price sky-high. Or should she keep Lundborg and his power, whatever it was, for her own evil? That would serve The Boss right. How much could it cost to keep Lundborg caged and barely fed? Malevia pictured herself as The New Boss. Then it would be payback time for that traitor Claude.

She hurried to the headquarters trailer to run the analytics on her laptop. As usual her computer confirmed her instincts. Malevia called up an inventory of building supplies and did a quick design. On her bot tablet, she quickly coded a new program and punched *send*. Outside, the defensive secondary of her football bots unplugged themselves from battery chargers and whirred into action. Then she downloaded a file from the internet and sent it to her 3-D printer.

As the printer hummed, Malevia stared out the window, fine-tuning her plan. At heart it was simple: that idiot Lundborg would follow his sister. All she had to do was get Kirsten.

She swung her hip waders up on the couch and smiled grimly. She could already taste the first Chompo bar.

CHAPTER 17

SCHEME FOR A SILK SUIT

Claude poked his head out of Kirsten's backpack as she and Tex rode their yaks to base camp. *So this is Pianvia*, Claude thought. It was even more of a dump than Camp Pan-American or Dimly, Manitoba.

It had taken Claude less time than he'd thought it would to escape the owl. A few minutes after he'd been trapped in the downspout it had flapped off after something else. As he slipped away he'd caught a glimpse of it trying to peck a Frisbee to death. Despite the "wise old" reputation, owls were actually quite stupid.

Unfortunately, his satchel and clothes had been shredded. But Claude was used to travelling *au naturel*. A ride to town with camp counsellors out for the evening, a scramble onto a southbound rig stopped at the one traffic light, and from there it had been a snap to get to the airport. Instead of looking for Lundborg, Claude had done the only sensible thing: slipped on the next flight to Winnipeg, then a bus to Dimly and the sister, who would lead him to his goal. She was doing it right now.

"Pianvia," Claude had messaged The Boss. "What a coincidence." "Meet there," she'd messaged back. He knew Malevia Spleene was here too, somewhere. Now, surveying the dismal landscape, Claude reminded himself to forge double expense receipts. Then he listened as Tex talked about using Gary Lundborg's powers to disrupt a mountaintop redium mine operated by moles.

The news made Claude's whiskers tingle. Reidium was achingly rare. At Fassbinder's lab they had to extract tiny amounts of it from old Dimly Bulb gear. There was barely enough to mutate worms into anacondas. But with a mine full of the stuff you could rule the world. It looked as if The Boss had found one.

But it also looked as if Department C was planning to steal the reidium for Fassbinder. Claude could be the game changer here. The question was, which side should he help?

The Boss was evil, vicious, untrustworthy, and had

terrible taste in disguises. Fassbinder and Department C were dedicated do-gooders, out to make the world a better, safer place. Unfortunately the pay was terrible and the working conditions lousy. Claude was sick of that miniature minigolf course and the ancient computers. Plus, no one liked his reality TV idea except that rat, Gerald — and he was long gone.

The Boss, on the other hand, would need someone with Claude's expertise to handle that reidium. And The Boss had promised he'd be rolling in cash. He'd sadly mention what happened to poor Nurse Nusswuss, or whatever her name had been, and his value would climb even higher. In fact, for his help, the price would be partnership: Claude and The Boss could rule the world together.

Or even better . . . Claude smiled. His decision made, he settled down for a cat nap (how he hated that term). He was glad he'd taught himself Pianvian on the flight over. There'd be a lot to do before The Boss's blimp floated in, but he had a feeling his next suit would be made of silk.

He woke as the yaks stopped. Claude peered out. They were at the foot of a mountain. The backpack was put in a shack, with a box of candy bars. He popped out, chewed through the cardboard, and nibbled on a couple for a snack, then searched the place.

In the basement bunker he scanned various drone video feeds on computer screens. *This has to be the CIA,* Claude thought; the big leagues. Department C could never afford this.

One screen showed Malevia Spleene, in hip waders and a parachute pack, standing on top of the mountain. Claude chuckled. She wasn't going to be happy to see him. He could hardly wait to spoil her day.

He scampered outside. A game he recognized as fleever was surging back and forth. Claude hopped onto a slow yak as it panted by, hoping for a lift close to the mountain road. Then something wonderful happened: there was an immense explosion and before he knew it they were riding toward Malevia Spleene.

Halfway up the road Claude realized the yak rider was a bot, lack of breathing being a big clue. At cliff's edge, they passed more bots, building something. He

hopped brazenly onto the yak's head as they rode into the mountaintop compound.

Malevia Spleene came out of her headquarters trailer. Her eyes narrowed. "You."

"None other," Claude buffed his claws. "You were expecting Santa Claus, maybe?"

"And where are your clothes? You're disgustingly naked."

"I prefer to think of this as *au naturel*. It's how I travel. On to more important matters: in case you didn't know, The Boss is on the way."

"Well, duh, you little rat. The garlic shipment is tomorrow."

Claude hadn't known about a garlic shipment, but he didn't let on. It would just mean working faster. He said simply, "Watch who you're calling a rat, Malevia. I'm in charge here now. And Lundborg is down in that pasture. When were you planning to tell The Boss?"

"As soon as she gets here. I only just found out myself. I'll have him caged in an hour, tops."

She? The Boss was a she? Claude was learning all kinds of things here. He didn't let on about that, either. Instead, he said, "I think you're lying, Malevia. I think you've known he was here all along, that you've been hiding him to trick us. I think you know his powers too. I'm telling The Boss you've been running a massive double-cross."

"What! *You* told *me* he had no powers, you—" Malevia spat out a stream of bad language that even the lab rugby team would have blushed at.

Claude didn't turn a whisker. "We're wasting valuable time. I can tell The Boss you were tricking her, and she can let her cats toy with you. Or, you can cut a deal with me and save your bacon. I'll even give you Lundborg."

"I'd be a fool to trust you."

"You don't have any choice."

Malevia scowled. "Start talking."

"You first," said Claude. "Where's the reidium and where are the moles?"

CHAPTER 18

A VILLAIN'S WORK . . .

The Boss crossed *Yell at Clutterbucket* from her To-Do list. With four superpowered children to control and multiple nefarious schemes, minions were a necessary evil. But sometimes they drove her crazy. Greep had gotten herself jailed fighting with Jess, Clutterbucket was slow as molasses dealing with Archie, and Bafflegab would be clueless without that rat Gerald.

She pulled off a clown mask and ran a towel across the nothingness above her neck ruff. Those masks got hot. Cats lazed on her desk. Outside the window The Boss could see the vast Pianvian swamp as the blimp chugged on.

If Lundborg was in Pianvia, it meant Department C

was on to her reidium project and was trying to use him somehow. Claude had been vague about Lundborg's powers but clearly they were impressive. All the better.

Department C, she knew from Fassbinder's complaints in the old days, was famously cheap and klutzy. They were assigned only the problems no one else would take seriously. It would be a piece of cake to snatch Lundborg and obliterate whatever other losers were there with him.

In about twenty-four hours Lundborg would be in her clutches and everything — and everyone — would be taken care of. It would only be a matter of time till the other three children were under her control as well.

But now, a quick perfume spritz and back to work. There were still Greep and Bafflegab to scream at and the Cat-A-Tonic gas dispenser to top up. So little time, so much evil: a villain's work was never done.

CHAPTER 19

A CHOCOLATE BAR TO DIE FOR

After lunch, Sergeant Muldoon and Tex began feverishly recoding computer programs for the new plan. Gary and Kirsten left the hut. They emptied the dirt-filled pencil cases, then walked across the yak pasture, trundling the fake yak along behind them on a rope. The rollers on its hooves jolted over bumps and ruts, creating a surprisingly good imitation of walking. They parked it in its old spot by the mountain.

"So Mom and Dad still think we're at camp, huh? I wish I was," Gary confessed. He was still badly embarrassed about his mistake with the pencil cases. He was also worried that he wouldn't be able to make the new plan work. He took his glasses off and tried to twist the frames straighter. "I don't know about this school bus thing, K."

"Whatever." Just now, Kirsten was not her usual sympathetic self. She kicked at the grass. "I can't believe those guys wouldn't let me have one of their Chompo bars. They had a whole box."

"They were gross anyway. A mouse must have got into them. Besides, you don't even like Chompos."

"I do now," Kirsten said. "Did you see that video?"

Gary tried to remember. "I dunno. It's been busy."

"Never mind," Kirsten said. "There's something else I have to talk to you about, where they can't hear us. Something weird was happening back home."

"Is Dad still cleaning up all those slime puddles?"

"Not that," Kirsten said. "It's—"

When she didn't finish speaking, Gary put his glasses back on and looked up. In front of them, a wooden pallet was descending on ropes. The ropes ran to the girdered arm of a crane, high overhead. In the middle of the pallet sat a Chompo bar.

"Now we're talking," said Kirsten.

The pallet touched down, and she went for the bar. The instant she climbed aboard, a net dropped around her and the pallet lurched back up into the air.

"Hey," Gary yelled. "Wait! Kirsten—"

He jumped for the pallet. It was already out of reach and rising fast.

"It's not even a real Chompo," Kirsten cried. "What the—"

Gary frantically tried to think Kirsten back, but he knew his power time had long passed. He watched helplessly as the pallet rose swiftly up the side of the mountain. Beneath it a banner unfurled. Written in big letters was a message: *To get sister back, come up ALONE.*

"Ga-ry!" he heard Kirsten yell.

Gary turned and started to run.

CHAPTER 20

SPLASH 7 TO THE RESCUE

He raced along the base of the mountain to where the road began. He was starting up when he got the feeling: this might be a trap. He slowed to a walk. Above him the pallet dwindled as it approached the mountaintop. A few buzzards circled it, then flapped away. The message had said to come alone, but what he needed was help.

When he panted into the hut, Tex and Muldoon were still in the bunker, Muldoon clicking at a keyboard, Tex munching on a Chompo bar. "They're not really that good," he was saying. "Why did we want them so badly?"

"They grabbed Kirsten," Gary interrupted. "She was chasing a Chompo bar. We have to save her."

Gary blurted what had happened. Tex swivelled to a laptop. "What video feeds have we got?"

"They're all coming back up now," Muldoon answered. "Four and seven already good to go."

Tex pecked rapidly at his keyboard. "Sit down, Gary. We've got to do this right, not go off half-cocked."

Gary remained standing. "How many guns have we got?"

"Bullets are not always that helpful against bots." Muldoon turned to him. "For maximal damage what you really want are water guns or a firehose. You get a bot's circuitry wet and it's game over."

"Do we have any?"

"I've got a couple of Splash 7s in the munitions locker," Tex said. "I always bring 'em, just in case. But we also have to deal with Spleene, remember. And we don't want that reidium blowing up, or it'll be game over for all of us. Let's have a look at what's going on up there, first."

Video popped up onscreen: Kirsten stood in the mining compound. Massive bots on either side pinned her arms. In front of her, Malevia Spleene paced and waved her arms as she talked. Kirsten shook her head. Malevia Spleene seemed to laugh. Then she pulled a tablet from her pocket and stabbed at it, and the bots began to march Kirsten toward the shipping container.

The video dissolved into a pixel snowstorm. Tex swore and clicked the mouse. A moment later the picture returned, from a different angle. Now the bots stood before the container entrance. Kirsten was gone.

"Imprisoned in the container," Tex said.

Malevia Spleene was turning wildly, tapping at the tablet. Bots marched.

"They're going on high alert," Muldoon said. "Expecting us, I bet."

"I don't care," Gary said. "Let's go." He stood up.

"Whoa there, pardner," Tex said. "Stan's right. They're expecting us. This may not be the time."

"What are you talking about?" Gary snapped. "Let's go before they're ready."

"Gary," Muldoon said gently, "I don't think you understand. We're here to do a job, a very important one. Nothing can stand in the way of that; right now, not even Kirsten. You're the key to that job. They want you up that mountain. Going there is the worst thing we could do."

"But what about my sister?"

"We can try to build a rescue into tomorrow's plan. I'm pretty sure they won't do anything to her. She's too valuable to hurt — unless they get you."

"You're *pretty sure*? You'll *try*? She's got soccer camp next week!"

"Gary," Tex interrupted. "Like I said, this is not the time."

"*Then when is the time?*"

Tex sighed. "There may not be a time, Gary. If it comes to a choice between saving Kirsten and saving the world, you know where our duty lies."

Gary backed around the table. "I won't help anymore. I quit."

"Gary—"

"Unless we get her back. Now."

"This is hard for us all, Gary. But we have to do our duty. We'll do everything in our power—"

"So will I," Gary said. He shoved the table sideways, trapping the two men. As they struggled out of their chairs he flipped open the munitions locker and grabbed a lime-green Splash 7, then raced up the ladder.

"Gary!"

"Wait!"

Up in the hut he slammed the trap door shut and heaved the stove back into place over it. There was a rain barrel outside he could fill the water gun from. Gary flung open the door of the hut. Kirsten was galloping toward him on a yak.

CHAPTER 21

PART OF THE JOB

As the yak thundered up, Gary heard noises from inside the hut. The stove swung back and the trap door banged open. Tex and Muldoon scrambled up as Kirsten scrambled down.

"Gare," she panted, "I've got to—"

She stopped as the two men joined them.

"Good going, Kirsten!" Tex reached for a high-five. "How'd you do it, girl?"

"I'll tell you later," Kirsten scowled. "I wouldn't have had to do anything if you'd just shared your Chompo bars."

The men nodded and scuffed at the dirt. "Sorry about that," said Muldoon. "C'mon in and have one. Don't know what came over us."

They went in the hut. Muldoon handed an un-nibbled Chompo to Kirsten. She tore into it. "I never used to like these," she said.

"Tell us about it," Muldoon said. "You see that video too?"

"Never mind that," Gary said. "How'd you get away?"

Kirsten shot him a look. "Later."

"Kirsten's right," Tex said. "We can save that for the report. What's important is that now they know we're not Pianvians. This changes everything. I've activated the perimeter sensors. We'd better load the Splash 7s in case of attack." He reached for the one Gary held. "On the plus side, knowing we're not Pianvian doesn't tell them who we *are*."

"I think they know who I am," Gary said. He told about the message on the bottom of the pallet.

Tex gave a low whistle. "How the . . . ? All right. We might have to saddle up for an emergency evac and just call in the missile strike on the mine. Dang."

"Not yet," said Muldoon. "Cheeper and Fassbind-er set up a Skype session for today, remember? May-be they'll have something." He checked his watch. "Twenty minutes from now."

Tex nodded, then went to the munitions locker. He passed Kevlar vests to everyone, then began loading various weapons. The Splash 7s he passed to Gary. "Fill 'em at the rain barrel. Kirsten, I'd be obliged if you saddled the two yaks tethered out back."

"Only two?" Kirsten asked.

"If necessary I'll call in a chopper for you two. Stan and I will stay here to cover your retreat. We can't let them get Gary."

"But what about you guys?"

"Staying here would be part of our job."

Gary felt something go very cold inside him. He took the water guns outside. As he filled them he looked at the mountain. Even the buzzards were still. A dirty brown blimp was approaching fast.

CHAPTER 22

A MOUSE CIRCUS AND FOUR TEENAGE WHACK JOBS

Muldoon brought a tablet up into the hut for the Skype session. After the usual fussing with connections, Bernard Cheeper and Dr. Fassbinder appeared onscreen, looking grim. They were in the lab. It looked as if people had been autographing the cast on Cheeper's arm.

"We think your mission has been compromised," Cheeper said.

Dr. Fassbinder nodded. "I'm sorry to say that it looks as if Claude, a key member of our research team, has gone rogue. He vanished a few days back. At first we assumed cat trouble; it's a hazard for my team. But when we checked his messaging, we found links to Malevia Spleene."

"And we all know who she is," Cheeper put in. "Which means The Boss, whoever that is, knows as well."

"Roger that," said Tex. "We already knew Spleene's on to us. Now we know how she found out. She just tried to snatch Kirsten to get at Gary. The question is, how much do they know about Gary's powers?"

"Claude knows it all," Fassbinder's moustache flared. "But he's a wily one. We think he was also pitching a reality-TV show. He was definitely playing online poker and the stock market. How much he's told anyone and what their agreement is, is anyone's guess."

Cheeper said, "We have to assume the worst. And we can't let Gary fall into their clutches. Department C advises scrubbing the mission."

"That reidium would have changed everything," Dr. Fassbinder sighed. "We're on the verge of big breakthroughs. A lifetime's research . . ."

"Gary isn't ready," said Cheeper flatly. "Given his, ah, problems with . . ." he waved his cast at the camera. "You know that yourself."

"Yeah, I'm clumsy," Gary admitted. "I know everyone calls me Clumsborg. And I forget stuff. But I try. I did better yesterday . . . uh, for a while."

"Of course," nodded Dr. Fassbinder. "I knew you would."

"He saved our lives today," Kirsten put in.

"See?" said Fassbinder.

"All very nice. He still needs more . . . training," Cheeper said.

"Gary is a lot more capable than you think," insisted Dr. Fassbinder. "All my four are. You have to give them a chance."

Cheeper snorted. "What they are, is trouble. Their powers are ridiculous. Listen, C says cut our losses and launch a missile strike to destroy the reidium before Spleene and Claude and whoever else can get to Gary. Can you imagine what they'd do with his powers?"

"But you just said he can't control his powers, that he's ridiculous. What good would he be to them? You can't have it both ways!" Dr. Fassbinder waved his arms. "If you had just funded us properly in the first place none of this would have happened."

"*Funded* you properly?" Cheeper snapped back. "For a mouse circus and four teenage whack jobs? All the money I've gotten you on my tiny budget and—"

They were shouting now. They seemed to have forgotten they were Skyping. Gary cringed. He felt Sergeant Muldoon put a hand on his shoulder. "Fellas," Muldoon said soothingly, "this isn't solving anything."

Red-faced, Fassbinder and Cheeper turned to the camera again. Dr. Fassbinder smoothed his Grateful

Dead T-shirt. Cheeper straightened his necktie and cleared his throat. "Ahem, yes, anyway . . . Final call goes to the mission commander on the ground. Tex?"

Gary spoke up before Tex could answer. "I can do this. We can do this."

"Right on," he heard Kirsten murmur.

Tex looked at him. Was he remembering the mini-avalanche, how the reidium got sent back up the mountain, the way he'd disobeyed orders just now or the end of the fleever game? Gary got his answer. Tex said to the camera: "We'll carry on. FYI, there's a new game plan. The blimp has arrived and the timeline is forty-eight hours shorter, as I advised earlier. We're ready to execute. Have the exit chopper here tomorrow at eleven hundred hours our time. It will be mission accomplished by then."

"Eleven a.m. confirmed," Cheeper said, making a note on his cast. "Be careful and remember to bring out all your receipts."

"Roger that," Tex said dryly. "Thanks for the reminder." He closed the Skype link.

Muldoon winked at Gary. "We've got some practising to do."

Gary looked at Kirsten and thought, *No more Clumsborg. Game on.*

CHAPTER 23

PLOTTING MAKES ME HUNGRY

Meanwhile . . . Malevia watched The Boss climb down the rope ladder from her blimp, which hovered above them belching noxious black smoke. The Boss was dressed like a cartoon sponge and carrying a cat. After all the time she'd spent up here with moles, Malevia was almost glad to see a feline. And speaking of repulsive furry creatures, where was Claude? She hadn't seen him since she'd pointed him to the crate that was the mole bunkhouse.

Malevia still hadn't figured out just how Lundborg's sister had given them the slip, but she knew she had to tell The Boss that they were down there. If she didn't, that slimeball Claude would. So much for keeping Lundborg for herself.

To cheer up, Malevia reminded herself that she'd soon be out of Pianvia, munching on a Chompo bar, and that she could have her bots deal with Claude in some very painful way before she left. Plus she'd kept a couple of pencil cases full of reidium for herself. If The Boss wanted it so badly, there had to be a market for it somewhere.

"Reporting time, Spleene," said sponge Boss. The cat glared. A faint odour of burnt rubber wafted on the breeze. Malevia shrugged her parachute higher and said, "The reidium is packed and ready to go. The school buses are gassed up. The garlic train is on schedule. My bot team is programmed for the hijacking." Malevia thought she spotted the eyeholes in the sponge outfit. Strangely, they looked blank. She went on, "And I have a surprise for you."

"I don't like surprises, Spleene."

"You'll like this. I've found Lundborg. He's here, at the foot of the mountain. I've been keeping an eye on him till you arrived. Waiting for orders."

"Have you now? Does he know that you know?"

"He doesn't know that I know," Malevia lied.

"How do you know?"

"Trust me. I know that he doesn't know that I know. That he doesn't." There was a pause as Malevia tried to figure out what she'd just said. To fill the silence she added, "I'm assuming there's a bonus for this."

"Fat chance, Spleene. Claude already told me Lundborg was here. Where is Claude? The three of us need to have a meeting about tomorrow, pronto."

"He's with the moles." She couldn't keep the disgust out of her voice.

"I'm right here."

Malevia looked down. Claude was beside her. She fought back an urge to stomp him with a hip-wadered foot.

"And respect those moles," Claude sniffed. "Natural mining skills. Without them, we'd be kaput."

"Enough," growled The Boss. "Meeting. Now. In the trailer."

Malevia led them into her headquarters. The Boss let the cat roam and stood by the couch. Clearly the sponge costume made it hard to sit. Claude scurried up high, to the sill of the open window. Malevia gritted her teeth and moved to the whiteboard, on which she'd written out the next day's plan.

"Run it down," ordered The Boss. Malevia began to read aloud, making sure to highlight meals. Experience had taught her The Boss liked her chow. "Nine a.m.: load School Bus 1 with reidium. Nine-thirty a.m.: *light breakfast*! Ten a.m.: bots drive School Bus 2 down mountain; grab Lundborg; destroy everyone

and everything else. Ten twenty-five a.m.: bots drive Bus 2 to railroad tracks, then park across them to stop garlic train. Eleven a.m.: bots hijack train and load garlic onto Bus 2. Eleven-thirty a.m.: coffee break *with fresh muffins*! Twelve p.m.: Malevia drives Bus 1, with reidium, down mountain; meet Bus 2; convoy across border to Dystopia. Two p.m.: rendezvous with Boss and blimp in Dystopia; *catered picnic lunch.*"

"Not bad at all, Spleene." The sponge costume gave a little bend of approval. The Boss moved closer. The burnt-rubber smell grew more powerful. "There will be a couple of minor changes."

Malevia heard a faint hissing sound. Mist puffed from one of the sponge holes and the pungent scent of cat pee replaced the rubber smell. Malevia coughed. The Boss said, "I'll tell you about them tomorrow. All you need to know now is that my Cat-A-Tonic nerve-control gas will make things much easier."

"But," Malevia said, "my plan is—"

She felt oddly light-headed. She tried to remember what her plan was.

"Cat-A-Tonic is quite effective, as you're learning right now. Sit down, Spleene."

Malevia found herself sitting on the couch. She didn't quite know how she'd gotten there.

"Now pick up the cat and scratch under his chin."

Malevia picked up the cat. The order was impossible to resist. In a way she didn't even mind; it was oddly nice not to think.

"That's all for now, Spleene. Give me the cat, take off your parachute, and climb up to the blimp. Tell them I want lunch in half an hour. I may look like I live on air," The Boss gave out a raspy gasp that might have been a chuckle, "but plotting makes me hungry."

The next thing she knew, Malevia was climbing the blimp's rope ladder high into the sky. It seemed like the most natural thing in the world.

CHAPTER 24

DELICIOUSLY EVIL

When Malevia left the trailer, The Boss turned to Claude. She put the cat down. It dashed to the window. Claude backed up. Moving closer, The Boss said, "You already know about Cat-A-Tonic, Claude. We don't need it to understand each other, do we?"

Claude shook his head.

"You talked to the moles? The reidium is truly ready to ship?"

"It's ready. I persuaded them to work one more shift tonight to top up the load. They'll be busy."

"Excellent. For once Spleene wasn't lying. You've done good work, Claude. I told you there'd be a reward. You get on with these moles? Do you want to stay here and run the mining operation? The pay is excellent."

Claude groomed a whisker. "I'm sure it is, but the life expectancy is probably short. Department C knows about this place now. Anyway, I'm a city mouse. Paris might be nice. And as you can see, I need a new tailor."

"I noticed you were travelling light. Fine. A fresh challenge then. You'll ride with me tomorrow."

"It'll be an honour," Claude drawled. "I'll go check on the moles." He jumped out the window as the cat leaped and sunk its claws into the sill.

The Boss gathered the cat into her yellow arms and smiled inside her sponge costume. Sometimes she marvelled at her own talent for this kind of thing. The real plan was pure diabolical genius.

Tomorrow, she herself would drive Bus 1, with the reidium, stopping off to capture Lundborg, and destroy everyone else down there with the help of Cat-A-Tonic. Spleene would drive Bus 2 and her bots straight to the railway and hijack the garlic. Then the garlic would be loaded onto The Boss's bus before the drive to Dystopia. As they convoyed to the border, the time bomb on Spleene's bus would detonate, sending Bus 2 and its occupants into the oblivion of the Pianvian swamp. The Boss would continue across the border with Lundborg, reidium, garlic and Claude. After they rendezvoused with the blimp, Claude could amuse her cats as they journeyed to her new lab and test kitchen.

There would be no mistakes this time, not with four superpowered children enslaved and a race of super-cats breeding in the lab. Plus, she loved to cook with garlic. Feeling hungry and deliciously evil, she headed up to lunch.

CHAPTER 25

HUMANS ARE SO STUPID

Claude paused outside the window, heart racing, whiskers tingling. He hid beneath the trailer until he heard The Boss clump down the steps, then watched her shiny black booties crunch off across the gravel.

At the mine entrance Zoltan, the chief of the mole mining crews, was waiting for him. "All good," Claude said in Pianvian. "I told her you'd be busy."

Zoltan nodded. His whiskers drooped from his snout. To protect his eyes from the daylight he wore dark glasses made of tiny bits of wire and green plastic from a pop bottle. He looked sinister even to Claude.

"She suspects *nyet*?" Zoltan growled.

"Putty in our paws," Claude winked. "Humans are so stupid."

"Too true," Zoltan nodded curtly. "They don't even like a good earthworm." He plucked a pink wriggler from a box at his feet and passed one end to Claude. "Here, we share!"

"Just had lunch," Claude lied.

"Eat!" Zoltan bellowed. "Juicy! Good for digestion!"

Claude pasted on a smile and began to chew.

CHAPTER 26

WHACK-A-MOLE

Gary lay awake in his upper bunk. Was Kirsten awake too? All day he'd sensed she wanted to tell him something. There hadn't been time, and he couldn't whisper to her now either. Tex was crouched at the window, wearing night-vision goggles. Beside him a laptop showed their perimeter sensors. Weapons gleamed faintly. Through the window, Gary could see the blimp silhouetted against the moon.

Stomach knotted, he ran over and over what he'd practised that day, thumbs twitching as if he was still working the game controller. It had been hard, tougher even than *Gang of Greats*. He'd been so nervous not even Kirsten was much help. Dr. Fassbinder had said his coordination would improve, but it sure hadn't yet. *No more Clumsborg,* he reminded himself. *Concentrate.* He'd reminded himself all day too, but it hadn't helped. Mostly it got in the way of concentrating. Was the fate of the world really depending on him?

What had he been thinking about before? Oh yeah, *Gang of Greats.* Gary wondered if Jess Flem was playing now. What was up with her? Kirsten had said weird things were happening back home. Did Jess have some kind of power too? Cheeper had said four whack jobs. If Gary qualified, Jess did too, with her sweatpants, vampire complexion and streaming nose. And speaking of whack jobs, what about that guy he'd met in Dr. Fassbinder's office, the one whose hair turned messy when he switched from smooth to snarky? Was he one of them too? Hadn't he seen him again somewhere? What power could *he* have? Was hippie Daisy the fourth? There were too many questions.

What had he been thinking about before what he'd been thinking about? Oh yeah, *concen—*

Tex tensed at the window.

"What is it?" Gary whispered.

Tex relaxed again. "No worries," he whispered back. "Just moles, I think. There's a lot of wildlife running around. Must be the full moon. Get some sleep."

Gary sighed. How could you sleep when you knew you weren't coordinated enough to save the world? What had he been thinking about? Oh yeah, *four teenage whack jobs.* Was that like Whack-a-Mole?

And then he must have slept because the next thing he knew it was dawn and Sergeant Muldoon was gently shaking his shoulder. "It's time, Gary."

CHAPTER 27

BUZZARD AT TEN O'CLOCK

Breakfast was quiet. Gary ate as much garlic bread as he could, then popped in a breath mint. He was getting tired of both. By the time the meal was over his powers were beginning to kick in. To warm up, he cleared the table.

"*Almost* epic, Gary," Muldoon said, sponging coffee grounds off his Kevlar vest. "We're going to ace this."

"For sure," said Kirsten, wiping something orange from her eye.

"Sorry about that," Gary said.

"No problem. I like marmalade."

Tex had moved the computer gear up into the hut for the getaway when the mission was done. All the laptops were on the table. One screen was blank. The others showed video feeds from the drones hovering around the mountaintop. Everyone huddled to watch.

At 8:53 a.m. the screens showed the heavily armed bots lining up. At 8:54 a.m. Malevia Spleene stepped from the trailer, yawning and wearing her usual gear. At 8:55 a.m. a gorilla climbed down the ladder from the blimp.

"Think that's The Boss?" Muldoon wondered. "Or another stooge?"

Malevia and the gorilla spoke. Malevia worked her tablet. Four bots marched off and loaded the blue bins of reidium onto the first school bus parked at the open gate.

"Bingo. That's our baby," whispered Tex.

Malevia and the gorilla spoke again. Malevia shook her head. She waved her arms. A mist appeared in front of her and Malevia sagged into slow motion. She prodded the tablet. All the bots but two filed onto the second school bus. When they were aboard, the gorilla strode into the trailer. Malevia followed like a sleepwalker. The compound was still.

"Ahead of schedule," said Muldoon. "The bots will be programmed to detect motion coming in, not going out. Let's kick it."

"Game on," said Kirsten. "Ready, Gare?"

Gary made himself nod. He sat down at the blank

computer. Tex and Sergeant Muldoon manned the others, controlling the drones. Kirsten stood, a hand on Gary's shoulder.

"Remember," Muldoon said, "just like the simulations yesterday. Except this time it's your power that's running things."

"We got this," Kirsten murmured.

Gary clutched his thumbs, remembering yesterday's fumbles with the game controller. Computer keys clicked. His computer lit up with a split-screen video stream from the drones. One showed the inside of the reidium bus through the driver's window. The key was in the ignition, on a Catwoman key ring.

"Okay, Gary," Tex said, "do it. Just the way we practised. Steal the bus and drive it down the mountain."

Nobody needed to mention the bus could blow up Pianvia. Gary took a deep breath, felt Kirsten's hand on his shoulder. He settled his glasses. *No more Clumsborg.*

What came first? In the nick of time, Kirsten whispered, "Remember, don't start the engine yet. Just—"

Oh yeah. He thought down the brake pedal. Onscreen it sank to the floor. Holding it down, he looked at the gearshift on the dashboard, then thought it out of park and down to neutral. He took a mental grip on the steering wheel and eased up on the brake. The bus began to roll. The bots did not react. The bus was past the gate. Gary thought the wheel to the right. It took all his energy.

Beside him, keyboards rattled furiously. The road swung into view: an impossibly narrow ribbon of gravel with cliff on the right and nothing but sky on the left. A buzzard sailed by.

"A-one," Tex said. Then, "Dang, lost a drone." A corner of Gary's screen went blank.

"No biggie," Kirsten said, patting Gary's shoulder. "You got this, Gare."

"It's hard to steer. And I can barely keep the brakes on."

"This is the tough bit, remember?" Kirsten soothed. "Power steering and brakes kick in when you start the engine. Get around this bend, you'll be far enough away that they won't hear. After that, it's easy as pie."

Oh yeah.

The first hairpin turn was coming up. Gary rode the brake, tugged hard left, and inched the bus around a sloping curve that looked like something from a roller coaster. For a sickening instant he saw nothing but sky. His fingernails scored his palms as he thought-wrestled the wheel; his feet tromped the floor.

"Oh, wow," Kirsten said. "Here it comes. I can see the bus out the window."

Gary fought the urge to look and thought-turned the key in the ignition instead. A backfire echoed across the valley. Everyone winced. From far away an alarm began to whoop. "They're on to us up there," Tex warned.

Another section of Gary's screen went blank. "We've lost another drone," Muldoon said. "They're so low the buzzards must be taking them."

"Drive, Gare!" Kirsten urged.

The power brakes and steering kicked in. The brain strain eased. Gary let go of the brake. The bus shot forward. "Aah!"

"What—"

"Buzzard at ten o'clock!"

A black shape blotted Gary's screen. Then there was nothing. Kirsten clamped his shoulder.

There was a *POP*. And then they weren't there either.

CHAPTER 28

PAGES OF FEAR

They were *in* the bus, hurtling toward the edge of the cliff. Instinctively, Gary stomped the brake with both feet and yanked on the wheel. They skidded to a halt centimetres from the edge.

"What happened?" Gary gasped. The bus backfired again, rattling like a dice cup. Above it all, the alarm was deafening.

"I'm sorry," Kirsten wailed. "Gare, I'm so sorry!"

"Huh?"

"I–I've got this power," Kirsten stammered over the background whoop of the alarm. "It started at soccer. I wanted to be downfield and suddenly I was; just *there*, somehow. You can move stuff, right? Well, I can move *me* — and anything I'm touching. That's how I got off the mountain when they grabbed me. But I can never tell when it's going to work. It didn't when they first caught me, then it did."

"But you weren't — I mean — reidium . . ."

"I've had a Dimly Bulb night light in my room forever. It broke a while back and this glowy powder spilled out. And I accidentally stepped in it. And it got in this blister I had from my soccer cleats. And now I have to be careful what I wish for."

"You *wished* us here?"

"I'm sorry. I wanted to be where we could see to drive this thing! We've gotta go, quick, before the shaking blows up the reidium."

"Then do it. Get us out of here!"

"I'm trying. It's not working. Drive!"

"Huh?"

"*DRIVE!*"

"Oh, right." Gary froze. "But I don't know how to drive!"

"What are you talking about? You just did it!"

"*Huh?*"

"C'mon, Gare. You have to, to save us all."

Fighting a rising tide of panic, Gary stared at the dashboard. He wished he'd paid more attention all these years as his parents drove them around.

What came first? Maybe this: he grabbed the

gearshift and pushed it up to R. *Clunk.* He lifted his feet. The rattling stopped, and the bus rolled back from the brink. And crunched the cliff wall. The rear bumper fell off.

"Perfect," said Kirsten. "Let's roll."

Concentrate. What next? Forward. He braked, and spun the wheel away from the cliff's edge. The gearshift read *D 4 2 1.* D looked like a safe bet. *Clunk.* Up went his feet. The bus surged forward in a tight turn. Now they were *headed* for the wall. Gary yelled and wrenched the wheel. There was a *SCRAAAAAAPE* and another crunch, but they kept rolling, more or less in the right direction.

"Side mirror and front bumper," Kirsten said,

looking back. "No sweat. We're lighter without them." Then her voice changed. "Uh-oh. They're after us. Step on it, Gare!"

He cringed, but stepped on it. Lightly. The speedometer jumped to 40. It felt like 140. Gary's knuckles were dead white against the steering wheel.

"*Faster!*" Kirsten called from the back of the bus.

"I *can't* drive any faster, I'm only thirteen!" He wasn't sure what this meant, but it was all he had.

"You have to, they're gaining on us!"

The second switchback was dead ahead. The bus slalomed through the turn, Gary fighting the wheel. The road dipped like a roller coaster, then they rattled around another turn into a longer straightaway. Gary risked a look in the mirror. Through a dust cloud he saw the second bus fishtail around the bend after them. Bots leaned out the windows, weapons pointed.

"Boot it," Kirsten urged, running back to him.

He stepped harder on the gas. 50. 60. 65 . . . He looked in the mirror again. The other bus was still closing in. The gorilla was driving. Strange as that was, something even stranger happened. As Gary watched, it reached up with one hand and *pulled off its head.* Before his eyes the whole gorilla melted away. Nothing was behind the wheel.

"GARRRRRYYYYYYYYY!"

He didn't see the turn until the last second. Gary wrenched the wheel and hit the brake with both feet and all his telekinetic power. The bus swayed. Kirsten stumbled and grabbed him. Gary closed his eyes as they went into a sickening drift . . .

POP!

They were perched on the branch of a dead tree overhanging the road. Their bus stopped dead, centimetres from oblivion, as the second bus roared round the bend, its door open. Brakes screeched, gravel sprayed, and the second bus rocketed over the cliff, just missing theirs. Long seconds later several crunches and a *BOOM* sounded from below. Buzzards launched.

Kirsten scrambled down and ran to the edge. "Somebody's using a parachute," she called back to Gary. "I bet it's that Spleene."

Gary nodded. He was still thinking the brakes on. Now he thought the gearshift to P.

"Gonna drive it down?" asked Kirsten.

"Sure," Gary swallowed. "I think I have the hang of it now."

CHAPTER 29

TRUCKS AND BUTTERFLIES

For the rest of the drive they were too tired to talk much. Besides, Gary had to concentrate. Near the bottom Kirsten asked, "Do you smell burning rubber?"

"Maybe it's the brakes," Gary said. Then they were down and Tex was riding toward them on a yak. Sergeant Muldoon had ridden out to collect Malevia Spleene. Gary eased the bus through the pasture and parked it near the yak herder's hut.

"Chopper's due in fifteen minutes, a missile strike on the mine ten after that," Tex said. "Stan and I will offload the reidium as soon as he gets back. And you two: A-one job. I don't know how you did it and I'm not going to ask, but it was a privilege to serve with you." He snapped them a salute. Kirsten blushed.

Gary could feel his own face redden.

Tex had moved their gear outside. "Funny how animals know human behaviour," he said. "We're leaving and the place is already overrun with moles. Check around. We don't want to leave anything behind." He fanned a hand in front of his face. "Wow, you sure burned through those brakes, Gary."

Gary and Kirsten poked their heads into the hut. Tex was right. The place was alive. A mole darted down into the bunker. Another popped up out of the wood stove. "Cute," Kirsten said.

There was nothing left inside. They walked around to the back of the hut. A flash of yellow caught Gary's eye. Pushing aside some brush he saw a row of toy dump trucks.

"Hey, said Kirsten, "those were up on the mountain."

"Huh?" Gary walked over. The dump trucks were piled with bulging pencil cases.

Kirsten frowned. "What's this about?"

Gary shrugged. "They must be the ones I tried to send up there."

"Uh-uh, we emptied those yesterday, remember? Department C wants to reuse the cases."

"Oh yeah. But if the trucks were at the top, how did . . . what . . ."

Shouting sounded around the corner. "What is

this? Take off these handcuffs! You've got the wrong person. I've been kidnapped from a Mexican butterfly hostel! You can ask my parents; they run a charity."

Sergeant Muldoon was back with Malevia Spleene. He said, "I'm sure we'll straighten the whole thing out. How about you wait in here till we're ready to go." He put her in the hut.

A stream of curses erupted from inside. "YOU! I'LL GET—" Banging and crashing followed. They all peered in the window. Malevia was charging around the hut, stomping with her hip waders. Behind them, the bus roared to life and drove away. No one was at the wheel.

CHAPTER 30

A KNEW FEELING

"Gary," Tex said. "Not the time for kidding around. Bring the bus back. We still have to offload the reidium."

"But I'm not driving it."

"Gary. Cut it out."

"It's not me!"

"*What?* Well, can you stop it?"

"No. I can't see the controls."

The bus reached the road. "Look," Kirsten pointed. Overhead, the blimp was descending in a series of shuddery bounces, farting more black smoke. Grappling hooks and the rope ladder swung beneath.

The bus stopped. One of the blue bins bumped down the steps. Everyone winced.

"They're going to get the reidium," Tex breathed.

"Maybe I can get us there," Kirsten said.

"No," Gary yelled. "I got this."

This time, it wasn't even a feeling; somehow he *knew*. He spun to the bushes, thought out a pencil case, and fired it at the school bus as the blimp began to rise. The bins now dangled from the hooks, and the rope ladder hung empty but straight, as if weighed down. A hatch opened in the blimp's gondola.

Below, the pencil case hit the bus. It erupted. The shockwave buffeted the blimp, knocking loose one of the bins. Everyone but Gary dove as it hit the ground. Nothing happened.

From inside the hut they heard Malevia hiss, "I should have known he'd steal it." That was all she would say.

CHAPTER 31

THE EMPIRE STRIKES FLACK

Malevia slumped against the wall of the hut, watching for Claude and pondering her situation. Now that the Cat-A-Tonic gas had worn off she could think clearly.

On the upside, she was getting a fast, free ride out of Pianvia and there would be parachutes on the helicopter. But no rodents, thank goodness. As well, they'd given her a Chompo bar.

On the downside, it hadn't tasted that great and she was still hungry. Also on the downside, she'd lost her bots, and The Boss would be mad at her.

On the upside, the bots had cost a lot to store and run, and The Boss might be dead. That would be great, because The Boss was a whole other order of nastiness and now maybe Malevia could take over her empire, or at least the cat racing.

On the downside, could you ever know for sure if someone invisible was dead? And could she take over and run an empire from jail? But would she go to jail? She was only fifteen. And exactly what had she done that was against the law, especially in Pianvia? True, she'd tried to snatch Kirsten, but she could claim that was just a joke. These clowns had stolen *her* reidium and destroyed *her* bots. She might make a fortune if she sued.

Malevia sat up straighter and wriggled against her handcuffs. "This is kidnapping. You're all in deep doo-doo. I haven't done anything wrong."

"You want us to leave you here?" Tex drawled. He was fitting the reidium-filled pencil cases in the blast-proof trunk.

"Get me home and I won't sue you all for twenty million dollars."

"Huh?" said Gary.

Malevia breathed deeply, then regretted it. Lundborg smelled like a garlic-flavoured breath mint factory. "I'm only fifteen. You can't pin a thing on me."

"Oh, yes we can," Kirsten said. "Cruelty to animals." She waved her cellphone. "I got video of you trying to stomp on all those poor little moles. That's attempted murder."

"Malevia, Malevia," Sergeant Muldoon said, "co-operate and we'll put in a good word for you. With luck the judge will only sentence you to community service. For something like this, it'll probably be at some kind of shelter for small animals."

A needle of fear prickled Malevia. Sergeant Muldoon went on, "I know there's a wonderful one for legless dachshunds. They're lovely little critters. A good experience like that might change your life, before it's too late."

Malevia slumped again. For the first time since she'd watched the Wicked Witch of the West melt all those years ago she felt like she was going to cry.

CHAPTER 32

. . . IS NEVER DONE

Meanwhile . . . The Boss limped invisibly around her blimp office. Her backside hurt too much from the explosion to sit down, even with the rubber doughnut she'd put on her chair.

She was angry too. Through everyone's incompetence they'd lost the reidium and the garlic. She looked at the pile of pencil cases heaped on the floor, all filled with useless Pianvian dirt. This was Claude's doing. She should have guessed he was double-crossing her when he was nowhere to be found that morning.

Still, as a veteran arch-villain, she knew all was not lost. It never was. Lundborg would return to Dimly; she could try again. In fact, she was heading there now, for the payoff of a brilliant scheme at the outdoor hockey game on Dimly Field. After that, there was much to do about the other special children. For those projects she had more able assistants. Spleene had turned out to be a bumbler, despite her early promise. Claude . . . well, it was too bad about Claude. The mouse had talent, and ambition. But then so had Dr. Fassbinder all those years ago, when she was still Nurse Debbie Nussbaum. Mice or men, they all let you down in the end.

With a sigh, she looked out the window at a particularly dismal view of a Pianvian swamp. Why were they flying so low? The intercom crackled. *"Attention, attention: altitude loss. The explosion has punctured our nose. Please prepare for soft swamp landing."*

With another sigh, The Boss turned to her closet and got out the economy-sized bicycle tire kit, life jackets for the cats and her Creature from the Black Lagoon costume. She'd have to work fast to make Dimly by halftime at the game. Truly, a villain's work was never done.

CHAPTER 33

ALL THE EARTHWORMS YOU CAN EAT

Claude and the moles stayed beneath the stove in the yak herder's hut after the chopper had lifted off. A few moments later they heard the scream of an incoming missile that fell short of its mountain target. They felt the *thud* as it buried its nose in the dirt outside the hut. There was no explosion.

"Knew it," Claude sniffed. "I warned Department C. That's what you get when you buy second-hand missiles."

Everyone descended to the bunker. They were more comfortable in the dark. Claude turned to Zoltan. "They've got the reidium but you've got the mine and I've got the know-how. You say there's plenty of garlic?"

"Smell my breath!" bellowed Zoltan. "All is good!"

Claude had already smelled Zoltan's breath. "Excellent. The bunker will be our lab. They even left us some Chompo bars."

"Better with garlic," said Zoltan. "So, back up the mountain, and we dig!"

"Exactly, then down here we refine."

"And we use powers to take over Pianvia!"

"First Pianvia, then the world." Claude smiled. "And I can get us a reality-TV deal on the way."

Outside, there was a thunderous explosion as the missile detonated. The hut collapsed above them.

"What now?" Claude frowned.

"We are moles, we are miners. Here are even more earthworms. We feast! We dig! We triumph!"

Everyone cheered. Claude bit into a Chompo.

CHAPTER 34

FOR THOSE STILL ALIVE

The helicopter pilot had given everyone but Malevia recycled envelopes as they climbed aboard. No one bothered to open them until they'd seen the contrail of the missile streak by and heard the *CRUMP* of its explosion some moments later.

"Mission accomplished," said Tex. "I bet I know what this is." He tore open his envelope.

"Every year," chuckled Muldoon.

Each envelope held the same message, printed on the backs of old photocopies. The print was so faint it might almost have been invisible ink.

"I wish Bernie Cheeper would at least spring for a new printer cartridge," said Muldoon.

Gary read:

Gary Lundborg
YOU'RE INVITED!
If you're reading this you survived your mission.
Congratulations!
To celebrate a year of (mostly) successful projects, come to our midsummer potluck picnic for those still alive.
Let us know if you'll bring salad, sandwiches or dessert. (And also cheese.)
Looking forward to seeing whoever is left.

Bernard Cheeper,
Department C Projects Coordination

PS You can bring one guest.

"If you go, watch out for Cheeper's bean salad," Tex said. "Powerful stuff. It could float that blimp on its own."

The chopper banked over the swamp, the cases of reidium secure in the cargo netting below. Gary kept one hand on his now very crooked glasses. Far off, he could just make out the blimp. It seemed to be flying low. He wrote a quick message to Jess Flem, just in case: "Jess. BUMP mgt ber hoodinggg yarll wy. LOK FORRT IT!" Hmmm. He might be able to drive, but he couldn't say his typing had gotten any better. He hit send anyway.

"Dystopia in twenty minutes," the pilot's voice crackled in his headphones. Kirsten was taking pictures with her phone. Malevia Spleene was sulking. Tex was napping. Sergeant Muldoon was reading his *Be the Bright Side* book.

Gary settled back in his seat and had another breath mint. He guessed he wouldn't be home in time for today's big outdoor hockey game at Dimly Field. He wondered if the picnic was the same date as basketball camp. Could he ever get a pickup game at 4:00 a.m.? How long had he been away? Had he ever done his math homework? Had he ever had bean salad?

What had he been thinking about?

Oh yeah. Home.

Acknowledgements

I'm not the first to note that you write on your own, but a book is a team effort. And in this case, not just a book, but a series whose parts link and overlap, with Easter eggs tucked inside. Keeping things goofy and seemingly simple turned out to be a lot of complicated work. Luckily, that work was the most fun you can have without water balloons, thanks to some amazing people.

First, my Squad mates, Epicures all: Richard Scrimger, Kevin Sylvester, Lesley Livingston and Britt Wilson. Richard and I, old pals and no strangers to hatching plots together, first roughed out the idea for Almost Epic on a ride from a school presentation. Richard has been scheming persuasively about chocolate bars ever since. We knew exactly who we wanted to scheme with, too. To our delight, Kevin blew out some demented ideas and jumped aboard. Lesley drew no conclusions about our sanity and started talking pineapples and monsters (wait till you read all their books). Britt just nodded calmly and started to draw. You can't ask for more: true collaborators, true friends, and I'm privileged to work with them.

The horrendous task of keeping us all galloping in

more or less the same direction fell to Anne Shone and Erin Haggett at Scholastic, true friends also. Think of them as the calm coaching staff of our fleever team, who communicated with us even when we forgot to wear our earpieces, or left them on our yaks. Anne not only went to bat for the series when I first pitched it, but she juggled four writers, four plots, four timelines and countless bits of (mostly) inspired weirdness with her usual aplomb and an oddly Columbo-like manner (minus the trench coat). At the same time she gave me her usual deadly accurate advice about my writing and story. Erin somehow kept all the details, continuity, intersections, Easter eggs and schedules straight while pretending she thought this was all normal, which is way more than I could do. Thank you, thank you, thank you.

My thanks also to everyone at Scholastic for all their time, effort and enthusiasm. It's a delight to be in such good hands. (Another team!) And of course, my thanks also to David Bennett and now Amy Tompkins at Transatlantic Agency for their hard work delivering Almost Epic into those hands. It was hugely appreciated.

When people like me aren't scribbling, you often find us in schools, talking to kids about reading, writing and imagining, thanks to teachers and librarians. I owe many of them thanks, not least Richard Reid of the Durham District School Board, whose enthusiasm and imagination have been the catalysts for so many great events that we named reidium after him.

Finally, as always, thanks to Margaret and Will, who make every day more than epic.

TED STAUNTON is the award-winning author of over forty books for young people, including picture books, novels, non-fiction and graphic novels. Ted is a contributor to the popular Seven series and other recent books include *Bounced* and *Harry and Clare's Amazing Staycation*. A busy and popular presenter at schools, libraries and conferences across Canada, Ted is also a roots/blues musician in his spare time. Ted's personal superpower is an uncanny ability to forget names and song lyrics instantly. And many other things, too, probably . . .

FOUR BOOKS.
FOUR AUTHORS.
FOUR UNFORGETTABLE
SUPERHEROES.

What Blows Up by Ted Staunton
Hey, look, you're holding it in your hand!

Mucus Mayhem by Kevin Sylvester, available now
Jessica Flem is allergic to everything except video games.
She's used to a nose that never stops running, but is not
prepared for the mysterious power that shows up around
her thirteenth birthday. Could there be a use for all those
snot-filled tissues? She's about to find out . . .

Super Sketchy by Lesley Livingston, available May 2019
Daisy Kildare is starting over at a new school. Sometimes
she wishes she could be anywhere else. But when she uses
a certain pencil, Daisy finds she can *turn into* whatever she
draws. She just needs to harness that power. If only her
drawing skills were a little more accurate . . .

Irresistible by Richard Scrimger, available September 2019
Archie O'Kaye mostly rubs people the wrong way.
But when he becomes utterly charming right before
everyone's eyes at his thirteenth birthday party, his family
and friends know something is up. And they're not the
only ones watching . . .

Visit www.scholastic.ca/almost-epic
for chapter excerpts, videos and more!

Sneak Peek at *Super Sketchy*
by Lesley Livingston

A TALE OF ONE WEIRDO

aisy had never been able to talk about the annual treks from Dimly to Montreal with anyone other than Jess, who'd had to suffer through them every year too.

The whole thing was just too bizarre. Year after year, Dr. Fassbinder would perform a series of poky-proddy tests. Then Daisy and her mom would return home, where Daisy and Jess would exchange notes . . . and then pretend the visits had never happened as far as anyone else was concerned. Add to that Daisy's mom's *extreme* reluctance to talk about anything to do with Fassbinder or the Boredom Institute — or pandas — and Daisy just never brought it up. With anyone. Ever.

But for some reason, Daisy felt like she could confide in Kip. Maybe it was that they both had nutso grandmas. Or that he actually knew where — *what* — Dimly was. Or maybe it was that he was a little weird too, but seemed genuinely nice. Whatever it was, Daisy didn't get the impression Kip would turn around and snicker with his friends about her once she was gone. The fact that he didn't seem to have a lot of friends might have had something to do with that impression.

"The place reeks of Gorgonzola and garlic," Daisy said, trying to describe the weirdness that was the Boredom Institute. "And they have a serious pest-control problem. All you can hear when you're in the examination rooms is scurrying and squeaking. And *nothing* ever happens! At least, nothing *usually* happens."

"Usually?" Kip asked, leaning forward.

"Well . . . last time we were there," she said, trying hard to remember the details, "I had to fill out yet another weirdo questionnaire, only somebody had walked off with all the pens. I'm all hooked up to the machines and nobody's around, so I go into my knapsack to get my own. All I've got is this box of pencils from my mom's work . . ."

"And?"

"And, for the first time ever, something happens."

Kip leaned farther forward. "What?"

"I get a shock. From the pencil."

"The . . . pencil." Kip leaned back a little. "Okaaay . . ."

"Right?" Daisy shrugged. "It's *so* no big deal but all of a sudden the machine I'm hooked up to goes bonkers! Beeping and pinging and the needle zigzagging all over the graph paper like there's an earthquake."

"Weeeird . . ."

"*Right?* So I drop the pencil, and the machine goes instantly quiet. But the big mirror on the wall ripples — like someone's leaning on the other side — and the scurrying and squeaking in the walls gets *really* loud." Now it was Daisy's turn to lean forward. After all those months of not having anyone — not even Jess — to tell her tale to, the details came pouring out of her like a ghost story told around a campfire, weird and spooky-cool. "And then I can hear Fassbinder and my mom talking in the waiting room. Then they're yelling. Then the door opens, Mom busts in all crazy-eyes, grabs me, tears off all the wire-stickies — which, *ouch!* — hauls me out of the Institute, throws me into the car, and drives like a maniac back to Dimly. Like, non-stop."

"Non-stop? That's a heck of a drive!"

"I know!" Daisy nodded emphatically. "The only time she stops is at a Timmy's for a whole tray of double doubles. And then, get *this*, when we're walking back to the car, I see this . . . thing. In the sky."